D1795807

ABOUT THE AUTHOR

Joyee Flynn grew up in Chicago living in the same house all her life until she went left for college. Though she has a great life, she loves to get lost in fantasy that only books could bring. Her wide interest in reading is reflected in her writings. Currently Joyee lives with her dog, Marius, named after a vampire from Anne Rice's *Interview with the Vampire* series. She dreams of one day living out in Montana, enough land to have a few horses, and find a couple of cowboys of her own.

A lover of men, Joyee's all about them in any form in her books. Vampire, werewolf, military, doesn't matter at all as long as they are hot, hard, and sex fiends!

WWW.JOYEEFLYNN.COM

WARRIOR CAMP

VOLUME 1

JOYEE FLYNN

Published by Silver Publishing
Publisher of Erotic Romance

LOVE'S DECEIT

WARRIOR CAMP, BOOK 1

JOYEE FLYNN

SILVERPUBLISHING
Published by Silver Publishing
Publisher of Erotic Romance

If you purchased this book without a cover you should be aware that this book is stolen property. It was reported as "unsold and destroyed" to the publisher, and neither the author nor the publisher has received any payment for this "stripped book."

SILVER PUBLISHING

ISBN 978-1-453848-75-3

Warrior Camp 1: Love's Deceit
Warrior Camp 2: Love's Indecision

Copyright © 2010 by Joyee Flynn
Editor: Alison Todd
Cover Artist: Reese Dante

All rights reserved. Except for use in any review, the reproduction or utilization of this work in whole or in part in any form by any electronic, mechanical or other means, now known or hereafter invented, including xerography, photocopying and recording, or in any information storage or retrieval system, is forbidden without the written permission of the editorial office, Silver Publishing, 17910 Chester Street, Detroit MI, 48224 USA.

All characters in this book have no existence outside the imagination of the author and have no relation whatsoever to anyone bearing the same name or names. They are not even distantly inspired by any individual known or unknown to the author, and all incidents are pure invention.

Visit Silver Publishing at www.SilverPublishing.info

Chapter 1

My name is Dimitri Anslow. I'm a warrior for my race and I'm in love with the best warrior in our camp, probably the world. The man I love is Alexander. Just Alexander, no last name. He's that badass and ancient he doesn't even have one. Alexander was born when people, vampires and humans that is, didn't have surnames, instead you were known by your first name and son of your father.

Alexander's origins are about as mysterious as the human icon Zorro's are. Everyone knows he is a legend, but it's almost taboo to ask anything more. The thick Russian accent gives away his nationality at least, but that is about it. Plus, the accent always turns me into horny goo.

When I first saw him over fifty years ago, it was lust at first sight. I know, it's supposed to be *love* at first sight. But I don't believe you can love someone without getting to know them first.

I was brought to the warrior camp when I was twenty-four, a year before my transition. I was the middle child, granted I was the middle of seven, and the only warrior born to the family. That in itself was extremely odd since there isn't even any hint of warrior lineage in my family. It's not all that hard to determine at birth if a vampire will grow to be a warrior or not. First, we're born early; I popped out of my mother after seven months, not the normal nine. Also, I was a large baby. My mother reminded me of this quite often, almost to the point of my feeling the need to apologize for it constantly.

It's common practice for people who are born of warrior blood to be taken to a camp. The warriors help train and prepare us for not only our transition, but also life after it. But none of that is really important, only Alexander.

My parents had just turned me over to the warrior in charge of the camp when I first saw him. To use words like stunning, gorgeous, hot, beautiful . . . well, they aren't enough to accurately describe Alexander. He's a *god*.

At six foot three, and with two hundred forty-five pounds of solid muscle and strength, what else could he possibly be? Not to mention his glorious jet black hair that curls just around his shoulders if he doesn't have it pulled back. But nothing compares to his hypnotic sapphire blue eyes. Alexander doesn't smile much or even show emotion at all, but I've learned his eyes say everything in his heart without a word. Even more alluring is how his eyes turn silver when he's pissed off or about to fight.

For decades I've kept far enough away from him to

make sure he doesn't know how I truly feel, but also close enough I can always watch him from a safe distance. Makes me sound like a stalker, but I can't even help caring. That all changes today. Today, I will give myself to him.

The warrior camp isn't like ancient warrior camps were, though there are still some of the old traditions. It's more like a human military base, but it comes complete with battles for dominance as of old. A warrior can challenge another for several reasons. One being to show they are now stronger and willing to fight for a higher rank amongst us. Or it could just be an everyday argument that results in a challenge.

Whatever the reason is for one to occur, challenge fights are not like normal sparring, ever. It's all about dominance and who is stronger, better. You can either take the challenge or yield. If someone yields they acknowledge their opponent as superior and higher in ranking than themselves. If a challenge is accepted the combatants fight until someone is defeated. The loser not only gives their rank to the winner, but their body as well.

To put it bluntly, the winner has the right to fuck the loser. It's a part of the older traditions, showing the winner is not only the strongest and best, but also demeaning the loser in public, stripping them of their rank and dignity. It's hard to hold onto any shred of pride when you lose a fight and immediately get fucked on your hands and knees in front of all the spectators.

Carefully, over the last decade I've challenged and fought my way up the ranks. I have yet to lose a single battle, but I also refuse to fuck someone in a crowd. The winner has the option of taking their prize in public or private. I always choose private and then let the loser off the hook so long as they swear by blood they will not tell a soul. It's worked so far, no one seems to know that I'm still a virgin.

Today that changes. I challenged Alexander. Now that I have worked my way up the ranks and am second only to him I am able to do so. Do I have a chance in hell of winning? Fuck no. But that's the point, I don't want to win against him. I want to lose so I can finally be with him, even if it's just one time.

* * * *

Alexander walked into the ring just moments before the fight was to begin, looking as calm and collected as ever. Even in the normal running shorts and sleeveless t-shirt we all wear he was stunning. He turned to me, and I tried not to swallow my tongue as he pulled his shirt off over his head. No one has abs like Alexander, or such a sculpted chest. I grasped my sword tighter to remind myself why we were here.

"I knew this day would come, Dimitri," he said to me as he tossed the shirt off to the side, and gripped his sword.

"You did?" I asked looking into his eyes. *Did he know all this time that I love him?*

"Dimitri," Alexander said, tilting his head to the side with a smirk on his face. The look on his face and tone in his voice made me feel as if he'd caught me with my hand in the cookie jar. "You have always been an apt student, training harder than any other warrior I have ever known. You've been fighting your way up the ranks at a remarkable rate. Of course I knew you would be challenging me soon."

"You know I mean no disrespect, Alexander," I said gently, wanting to touch him with every fiber of my being. And I had to say something so my relief that Alexander was unaware of the real reason I challenged him didn't show on my face. "I will always feel that you are superior to me . . . I just have to know."

"I understand, Dimitri," he replied nodding with a smile. "I was standing in your shoes myself, once. A long time ago. You have to know if you have surpassed the teacher."

I felt myself nodding, too afraid to speak.

"That doesn't mean I'm not going to wipe the floor with you," Alexander said laughing. I felt his laugh crawl over my body. It took everything I had not to shiver at the feel of it. Instead I turned around and leaned my sword against the post of the ring. I pulled my own shirt off, desperately trying to rein in my hormones. It was pretty much useless since just the sight of Alexander had my cock throbbing in my shorts.

"I'm ready," I said, turning back to him after grabbing my sword.

We faced each other, the normal ten feet apart. With our swords in our right hands, we held them against our stomachs and chests at an angle so the top of the weapon hit our left shoulders. We both bowed ceremoniously, out of respect to each other and the fight to come. In a flash we were both in fighting stances, swords raised over head, elbows and knees slightly bent.

Alexander struck first and I met his attack with my sword. Swords meeting in battle don't make the clanking noise sound engineers use in the movies. It's almost like a very large tuning fork. Every time the swords hit there is that loud crashing sound but they each reverberate until they are hit again.

If I wasn't concentrating so hard on not getting my

ass handed to me I would have just stood there and watched Alexander in action. He was truly amazing. I never even had a chance to attack him, he always kept me on the defense. I blocked swing after swing of his sword, feeling the collision through my arms and shoulder. Alexander was so much stronger than anyone I had ever fought before. After only five minutes of our fight sweat was pouring from me and my body was screaming in agony.

Only once I was sure I had lasted longer than anyone I'd ever seen Alexander fight did I let him knock my sword out of my hands. Immediately I dropped down on my right knee with my head bent, signaling I acknowledged my loss. Seeing Alexander's feet and sword come into view, I knew he was standing right in front of me.

"Leave us," Alexander said loudly to the crowd. "I wish to claim my prize in private."

I closed my eyes in relief at the fact he'd demanded privacy, as he always did before he fucked the man he bested. Kneeling there, waiting for the crowd to leave and Alexander to make his move, I shook with anticipation. The moment had finally come to be with him. But what he did next, I never imagined happening in a million years.

"Part of me is sad, Dimitri," he said gently once we were alone, as he dropped his sword and knelt before me.

He took my chin in his hand and raised it so I could look into his amazing eyes. "While it is not in me to lose a challenge or indeed any fight, part of me was rooting for you to win."

"Why?" I asked in a whisper, still trying to control my ragged breathing from the exertion of the fight. "Why would you want me to win?"

"You have trained so hard, and are the finest warrior I have ever battled," Alexander said, looking into my eyes.

It wasn't just his compliment that made me blush, but his touch and the realization that his body was so close to me.

"I have cheered for you from the sidelines of all your fights."

"I didn't know that," I answered, trying to turn my face away from those knowing eyes. I couldn't break his grasp on my chin without hurting both of us, so I didn't fight it.

"You fought valiantly, Dimitri," he said quietly, his face mere inches from my own. My pulse raced as I fought not to lean forward and claim his full, wet lips. "I release you for your obligation to give me your body."

"Wait . . . what?" I asked, snapping out of my lustful thoughts. "You can't do that."

"I can, and I am," Alexander replied looking at me as if searching my face. "I have never taken anyone I have bested. Sex against someone's desire is not something I want."

"No, no," I stuttered, realizing he was more honorable than I knew. While I adored him even more for his honor, I couldn't let him spoil my plan. "I can't be disgraced that way. I am not unwilling. I knew the consequences of my challenging you and I give myself freely. You won, Alexander, please do not shame me this way."

"Is that how you truly feel?" he asked, surprise written all over his face. "That I would shame you by not fucking after you lost this challenge."

"Yes, yes I do," I answered nodding my head rapidly. "I lost because you are the better man, the better warrior. It would shame my pride to not give you what you have won. I will not have my honor questioned when I knew what I was risking to challenge you."

"If that is how you truly feel . . ." Alexander said, still searching my face as he let go of my chin.

"It is, Alexander," I replied swallowing loudly. "You have won. I give myself to you unreservedly."

"I have never engaged in sex after winning before," Alexander said. I could almost see the wheels spinning in his head as he thought about the turn of events. "But if this is what you want, if you feel my denying your body will disgrace you, then so be it."

"I do, it is bad enough I lost the fight, I will not cower and deny what your gallantry has won," I replied quietly. He simply nodded, and I turned away from him to pull off my shorts. I was forever grateful he had been watching my face and didn't seem to notice how hard my cock was from the idea of him fucking me. Once the shorts were off I leaned over from my kneeling position so that I was on all fours in front of him.

I took a deep breath, closed my eyes, and thanked whatever powers that be that Alexander had not denied me. Just then I felt him kneel between my legs, one hand running over my ass as the other went to my waist.

"I will not hurt you, Dimitri," he said gently as he leaned over me and kissed my shoulder.

"I know you won't," I hissed as he hands moved the cheeks of my ass apart. Alexander slid a finger into my ass, probably having used his own saliva as lubrication. It went in easily, as did the second finger that followed. I bit my lip so hard I tasted blood so I would not groan in pleasure.

"You are prepared, Dimitri," Alexander said, the surprise in his voice apparent. I had taken the time before the fight to stretch myself, not wanting a single moment with Alexander to be ruined. What I hadn't thought of was that Alexander would take the time to do it himself. "Why are you prepared for me, Dimitri?"

I couldn't answer him, it would give away my secret. So I merely shook my head, hissing when his fingers left my ass. A moment later I felt the firm head of his large cock brush against my puckered hole and I shivered.

"Answer me, Dimitri," he said with a groan as he started to push his cock into me. The tone of his voice had me turning to look at his face before I could stop myself. Seeing the look of pleasure on his face, not to mention the lust in his eyes, is the only excuse I have for what I said next.

"Because I've wanted your big cock in my ass from the moment I saw you, Alexander," I answered blushing. I felt him freeze, his cock more than halfway into me.

"Is this true?" he asked giving me the full force of that gaze.

I opened my mouth to answer, but nothing came out. After two more tries, I simply closed it and nodded.

Alexander smiled widely and the look in his eyes became almost feral, possessive. "Well, if you have waited fifty years to be with me I had better make it good." Before I could even reply he slammed the rest of the way into me. I couldn't even hold back the moan this time. I had never been taken before, so no matter the amount of prep there was still that bite of pain with the pleasure. He slowly pulled his cock out until only this head remained in me, then started to push back in.

"Dimitri, am I your first?" he asked, shock on his face. Instead of answering, I turned away from his knowing eyes and pushed my hips back so that his cock slammed into me again. He gripped my hips to hold me still, "don't do that, I don't want to hurt you."

"It doesn't hurt, it feels amazing," I groaned even louder as his hands stroked my hips and ass. "Fuck me Alexander, make me yours."

"Answer me first."

"Yes, you are my first," I whispered, swallowing loudly before looking over my shoulder at him. "I never wanted anyone but you. It's always been you, Alexander."

"Good," he growled, tightening his grasp on my hips. I wasn't sure what he meant by 'good', but before I could ask he took me at my word and started fucking me. He started fast but gentle and his words alone almost made me come. "Is this what you imagined, Dimika? Or am I not as good as your fantasies of me?"

"Better, so much better than I ever imagined," I moaned in between thrusts. And it was the truth. His cock was slamming into my ass, rubbing my sweet spot every time. I felt like I was going to die from all the sensations running through my body. I didn't fight them, instead I rode the pleasure, knowing Alexander would catch me. "Oh god, Alexander. Harder. Fuck me until I can't walk, brand me as yours."

"My pleasure, Dimika," he hissed as he moved his hips even faster. I knew Dimika was a nickname for Dimitri, but no one had ever called me it before. I felt my heart race and my toes curl with pleasure at hearing it from Alexander. "I'm going to fuck you until you will never want another cock inside you. You will always want me, Dimika, and no one else."

"Yes, only you, Alexander," I cried as I tilted my head to the side, baring my neck to him. "I'm yours forever."

"Mine, yes, you are mine," Alexander growled as he leaned over and licked the side of my neck. The feeling of his fangs grazing my neck as he pounded into my ass was all it took for me to climax.

"Alexander," I screamed as my cock erupted, shooting cum all over the ground. He thrust into me faster as he roughly grabbed my hair and pulled my head down, away from him.

"No, I will not claim you," he grunted. I know he said it to me, but it almost sounded like he was telling himself. He stiffened behind me an instant before slamming into me one last time and roaring out his own release. After he collapsed on top of me I slowly lowered both of us to the ground. I was careful to make sure his cock didn't slip out of me. I needed to keep him here, with me, in me, as long as I could.

But I also wanted to see him and curl into his arms. The answer seemed apparent when his cock softened and slipped out of me. I reached behind me and held him to me as I turned so that he ended up lying on my chest. It didn't even occur to me I was basically rolling over in my own cum. All I wanted was to hold him, touch him. This might be my only chance with Alexander and I had to make the most of it.

"You dishonor yourself, Dimika," Alexander hissed as he raised his head off my chest. I instantly stopped stroking his hair and raised my head to look into his eyes. The look I saw made me gasp. Alexander was pissed off. If I couldn't tell from the ferocity of his gaze, the way his lips pulled back over his fangs was a dead giveaway.

"How did I do that?" I asked quietly, stunned at his reaction. I didn't understand. Why was he pissed after what we just shared? It was the best moment of my life, and he was pissed off? That sooo didn't seem right to me.

"You tried to trick me," he snarled as he pushed

himself up off of me.

"I'm sorry, Alexander," I whispered, trying to keep back the tears that were forming in my eyes. "I didn't throw the fight. You really did win, I couldn't beat you."

"I'm not talking about that," Alexander snapped as he reached for his shorts. "I mean during the sex. You tried to trick me into claiming you. You used the heat of the moment to try and bind me to you for all eternity."

"I didn't, I swear," I replied as I felt the shock of his words wash over me. That wasn't part of the plan, when had I done that? "I never even thought to try and have you claim me, you have to believe me, Alexander."

"Then why say you were always mine?" He asked with a smirk, clearly not believing me. He pulled his shorts on so roughly I was surprised they didn't rip. "Why did you tilt your head and bare your neck to me?"

"I am yours," I said, sitting up and reaching for my own shorts. Suddenly I needed to not be naked around Alexander anymore. "I didn't realize I was offering myself to you like that at the time. I-I didn't even think about you claiming me. It just felt right. I'm sorry."

"You mean that, don't you?" Alexander asked, turning that all knowing gaze on me and searching my face for the truth. I looked straight into his eyes and nodded as I pulled my own shorts on. I never meant for it to go this far.

"I would never try and trick someone into being my mate," I answered, still nodding like an idiot. "I don't want someone who doesn't want to be my mate. That wouldn't be fair to either of us."

"Good," he replied as he bent to pick up his sword. "You need to be more careful with any other partners you might have, Dimitri. I realize it was your first time, but you can't get swept up in passion and forget yourself like that."

"I don't want anyone else. There won't be any others," I whispered quietly. I knew the only reason he heard me is because of our excellent vampiric hearing. "I wouldn't have done that with anyone but you, Alexander."

Then he did the worst possible thing he could have as a response . . . he laughed. Alexander laughed so hard it took him a few minutes to recover. I had to turn away from him, the pain swelling in my chest became too much.

"You are still young, Dimitri," he finally chuckled. "You don't know what you want."

"I am not a child," I snarled turning back to him. "Don't tell me I don't know my own feelings. I'm not that twenty-four year old boy you met half a century ago, Alexander. I'm over seventy-five years old. Most humans are mated with children and grandchildren by that age. This is not some school school-boy crush."

"Call it what you like, but you don't know any

better," he said as he waved off my response like it was a pesky fly. I never once, ever, have been mad at him before. Always I respected and loved Alexander. I was so pissed off in that moment I was surprised steam wasn't coming out of my ears. I stormed over to him and grabbed him by the shirt he had just put back on.

"Don't brush away my feelings like that, Alexander," I snarled as I picked him up off the ground to put us at eye level. Even at the height of six foot three I still have five or so inches on him. "I love you. I know I love you, Alexander. It might have started out as some school-boy crush but it grew into something more. I love you more than I love myself, more than anyone else in the world."

"That's not my fault," he said, narrowing his eyes at me in anger. "I never asked you to love me. I don't love you, I don't even want you, Dimitri."

I dropped him to his feet so fast, as if touching him burned my hand. "It's no one's fault how I feel, Alexander. I can't help the way I feel about you. But don't laugh at me or my feelings."

"Fine, I won't laugh at you," he replied as he straightened his shirt and retrieved the sword he'd dropped. "Either way, it doesn't matter. I don't want you. We will never be mated. You need to move on to someone else, someone who will return your love."

I didn't even have the chance to reply because he spun on his heel and stalked out of the ring.

Not that I could think of a damn thing to say at that moment anyway. I was too busy holding my hand over my chest as if to keep my breaking heart inside my body. Right at that moment I wished he had killed me in battle instead of fucked me after it. Right at that moment I hated Alexander for being so cruel to me. Right at that moment, I hated myself for being so stupid and loving him.

Chapter 2

That night, as I showered myself, I scrubbed as hard as I could in scalding hot water. It was if I was trying to wash the anguish I felt off of me. No matter how hard I scoured I couldn't get rid of it. I felt like a character in Hamlet, *"Out damn spot."* But nothing worked.

Finally I just gave up and crawled into bed. Never had I felt so alone, so lost, in my own bed before. It was like, even though we hadn't had sex in my bed, I missed his presence. I did something that night I can't ever remember having done before . . . I cried. I cried so hard and for so long exhaustion finally overwhelmed me and I slept.

As if things couldn't get worse, I dreamed of being with Alexander over and over again.

"You will always want me, Dimika, and no one else."

"Yes, only you Alexander . . . ," I cried as I tilted my head to the side, baring my neck to him. *"I'm yours forever."*

"Mine, yes, you are mine," Alexander growled.

It played out just as it had in real life until that

moment. In the dream though, instead of pulling my neck away from him, he bit me. Alexander plunged his fangs into my neck and claimed me. In the dream, he made me his for all eternity. As only true mates could.

I awoke with a start, my hand going to my neck, frantically trying to find where he bit me. Then reality hit me like a ton of bricks. He hadn't claimed me, not really, only in the dream. I sunk back into bed, wiping my eyes before I started to cry again.

Why had he told me I was his if he really didn't want me? Was it some game to him? He didn't want me but he didn't want anyone else to have me either? He seemed like he wanted me so badly at the time . . . but then why say he didn't afterwards?

I threw my hands over my face and screamed in frustration. Then, like a switch was thrown in my head, I laughed. Of course he didn't want me. Alexander could have anyone he wanted, why the fuck would he want me? I knew I wasn't bad to look at. I was six foot eight and over three hundred pounds of solid, toned muscle. I kept my blond hair shorter than his, and stylish, but still out of my face so as to not distract me in battle.

Was it something he saw when I was naked that made him not want me? I'd seen others in the group showers after training, I knew where I stood. I was well endowed, even for a man as big as I was. I rolled over and looked at the clock, realizing I had to get my ass in gear. Rank in the camp not only came with extra privileges, but also more responsibilities.

As third warrior in rank for the camp, I was only under Alexander and the council member who oversaw everything. Seeing as I was still young for one of our race they had agreed I should be in charge of the pre-transition vampires. I had never doubted that decision or the intentions behind it before.

As I got dressed now though, I wondered. Had Alexander set it up this way so I wouldn't be around the other warriors? But why would he try to seclude me from everyone else if he didn't want me? Thousands of questions swirled in my head as I left my room and jogged over to my first class. I desperately tried to push it all out of my head and put on my teacher façade.

Reaching the gym I quickly pulled open the door and walked inside as if I didn't have a care in the world. I almost smiled when I saw the other warriors leaning against the wall. Today was a demonstration day: how to fight off, and defensive maneuvers against, a pack of Zakasac. That was the term we used for the vampires who had crossed over to the dark side. The translation from ancient Slavic was 'the bringer of death' or 'to be bitten to death.' It seemed a fairly accurate term considering what Zakasacs were.

Zakasac were once vampires as we were, but they chose to take lives for the power it gave them. Unlike us, who drank blood for necessity. Our race had strict rules about killing humans or other vampires. The only way to become Zakasac is to drain someone completely. They might gain more strength and speed, but they gave up the sunlight and their souls.

Human myths of vampires stem from the Zakasac. Soulless demons who slaughter for the thrill of the kill, and burn in the sun or if they touch or hold items. They were why our race had warriors and the camps to train them. Our job is to protect, our race and humans alike, from the threat of the Zakasac.

"There will be a time when you find yourself outnumbered," I said loudly. Every one of my students immediately hushed and turned to watch me. Again it almost made me smile, how eager my students were to learn. "I'm not going to lie to you and tell you that you'll only face one on one combat. And I'm also going to tell what you should do if you find yourself outnumbered . . . you run."

I waited until the gasps of surprise and whispers quieted before I continued. "If you are outnumbered there is no shame in running. Zakasacs are stronger, faster, and more powerful than us. This is why we fight in groups, as a team, to overpower them and win. If you find yourself alone and about to be attacked, you run. You run as hard and as fast as you can. You run and live so that you may fight to see another day."

A hand went up in the middle of the class, they were seated on the bleachers to see the demonstration. I nodded at the young man, Nate, who was one of my best students.

"I mean no disrespect, Dimitri, but have you ever run?" he asked searching my face. As much as I wanted to lie and not disappoint their eager faces, this was a lesson they had to learn.

"Yes, I have, Nate," I answered nodding, ignoring the whispers. "I've never run and left one of our race or a human unprotected. Nor have I ever run when I had other warriors with me, or anyone injured. We don't leave people behind or unprotected. I would willingly give my life in the fight to save another. But when I've been out on my own and had a pack of Zakasacs closing in on me? Fuck yeah, I've run. We all have. That's why we're still alive."

"How could you run from your enemy?" Another boy yelled out without even raising his hand. I looked up and sure enough, it was Lance. If there was ever a student I wanted to take outside and kick the crap out of just because he deserved it, it was Lance. Born of a wealthy, older family, he had a silver spoon stuck in his mouth from his birth. Unfortunately, his attitude made me want to shove that spoon right up his ass.

"If I may, Dimitri?" One of the other warriors pushed himself off the wall. I knew without even looking it was my best friend Matteo Dominguez. Even if I wasn't used to him always backing me up, his thick Spanish accent could never be mistaken. I nodded at him, giving him permission to address my class. "Listen up guys, because I'm only going to say this once. You are here to learn from us, we have centuries of experience in this room alone." As he took a pause to let his words sink in, Matteo looked intently at each of the students to drive his point home. "While we encourage you to ask questions, not a single one of you has any right to question us. Not our motives, our training, or our actions. If I ever hear anyone disrespect or question the honor of any warrior of the camp I will challenge them outright."

I had to bite my lip to keep from smiling as Matteo's words sank in and Lance visibly paled. But so like Matteo, he wasn't done yet.

"I don't care who you are or what family you're from. You're not with your parents anymore, you're here, and you belong to us. So, make no mistake about it, pre-transition or not, I will challenge you." He narrowed his gaze on Lance as he drove the message home.

"I will challenge you, you will lose, and I will fuck you so hard you can't walk, and I will do it in front of every warrior and pre-transition in this camp," Matteo growled. He was scaring the shit out of my students, but I knew Matteo better than that. He would never hurt or degrade any of the students like that. "Do I make myself perfectly clear, Lance?"

"Yes, Matteo," Lance answered at barely a whisper. The boy's face had gone so pale so quickly I was surprised he hadn't passed out.

"Good," Matteo replied nodding before turning his attention towards the entire class, not just Lance. "Dimitri speaks the truth. While no warrior ever wants to admit he has run, we have all done it. Running is why we are still alive. I don't care if you're just out of your transition or if you're centuries old like Alexander, we all have done it."

Just the mention of Alexander's name was like a knife to my chest. I managed to ignore it, until I heard his voice, "Matteo is right. I have run. What Dimitri teaches you is truth. You find yourself alone with the enemy approaching, you run."

I rolled my eyes and cursed the powers that be, of

course Alexander had to choose today to sit in on my glass. Seeing him leaning in the doorway out of the corner of my eye didn't help me stay calm. But I had a job to do. It was painful enough to think of him every waking second, I wouldn't let him distract me from my class, my teaching, and my job.

"Thank you, Matteo, Alexander," I said loudly nodding to each of them before I turned back to my class. "Today we're going to have a demonstration on what to do if you can't run. This isn't normal sparring or training. This is simply defensive maneuvers to help you get to the point where you can run. Never, ever, go on the offensive with a Zakasac pack. If they're too close for you to run, you defend and debilitate as best you can while you wait for your window to run."

I moved to the center of the gym where the mats were already laid out, pulled off my shirt, and threw it to the side. The six warriors who were helping me with the demonstration circled me as I moved into a defensive crouch. Two of the warriors lunged at me at the same time, exactly as we had seen Zakasac work in our battles. I kicked out hard at the warrior in front of me, then dove into a roll before the one behind me could land on my back.

My dive had two intentions, avoid my second attacker and take one of the others waiting by surprise. As I rolled to my feet I saw Alexander still leaning against the door, with a smirk on his face as he watched me. Immediately I was filled with such rage it was like its own living, breathing entity. I grabbed the next warrior who lunged for me by the arm and swung him so that he landed clear across the gym.

When the next one came at me, my mind was so clouded with hurt and anger I stopped seeing them as warriors. They were no longer my friends and fellow trainers, they were the enemy. I grabbed one of them and threw him hard into two other warriors, clearly catching them by surprise. One of them was brave enough, or stupid enough, to jump on my back. But then again, they didn't know I'd just snapped somewhere inside my head.

I reached over my head and grabbed the back of his shirt. In one single, powerful motion, I pulled him off me and over me. I kept the motion going until I slammed him on the floor so hard I heard something crack. When I saw someone else approaching me from the right, I picked up the man at my feet and flung him at my attacker. I didn't know how long we all fought, or the damage I had done until I realized no one else was attacking me.

Turning back to the class, I saw horrified, mesmerized looks of awe. Glancing around the gym, all six men lay unconscious and scattered. Fuck! I really had lost it. Alexander was still there watching me, but he no longer was smirking. He had a very serious frown on his face and it was directed at me. At first I started to feel bad that he was almost reprimanding me. Then I thought better of it. *Fuck him! If he doesn't like it, he can leave.*

"Does anyone have any questions?" I asked panting as I tried to control my breathing. Everyone in the class shook their heads. "Did this help? Do you now understand what we mean when we say defensive fighting and offensive fighting?"

I heard several of them say yes, and the others simply nodded while their mouths were still open and gaping.

"Good," I said, nodding like an idiot. "Then class is dismissed early. Everyone go head up to the mess hall. Except, Nate, come here for a second."

"Yes, Dimitri?" he asked after he climbed down the bleachers and walk over to me.

"On your way to breakfast, can you stop by the infirmary and tell them we need assistance at the gym?" I asked trying not to tip him off to the fact the demonstration hadn't gone according to plan.

"Of course, Dimitri," Nate replied, then jogged off towards the door. As everyone started to leave I turned and headed for the locker room. I knew I had to get my anger under control before the other warriors arrived and saw what I had done. Stripping off my shoes and shorts, I threw them in the direction of my locker and walked to the group showers. I turned one to full cold blast, not even flinching at the temperature as I stood under it, head hanging down in shame.

"You want to explain what that was?" Alexander asked, and I jumped, startled by the sound of his voice right behind me. Once again, we were talking while I was naked. Fuck.

As soon as I heard his wonderful voice, my whole body started shake. "I told everyone what it was, a demonstration on defensive fighting," I answered. I kept staring straight ahead at the shower tile as I put my hands on the wall to hold myself up. I really didn't think my knees were going to hold me up much longer.

"Don't lie to me, Dimitri," he replied. "Throw your bullshit somewhere else. I know you too well. You never lose control like that."

"I don't know what you're talking about," I said quietly. As if saying it softly made it less of a lie. "If I was so out of control, you would have jumped in and stopped me."

"Honestly, I was too startled by your behavior to react," Alexander stated. Just then I felt his hand touch my shoulder and again I jumped.

"Don't touch me," I snarled as I turned to face him and move out of his reach at the same time. "Don't you ever fucking touch me again."

The look of shock on his face was almost funny. He stood there, mouth agape, with his hand still stretched out towards me.

"I'm trying to shower here, Alexander," I growled. "You made how you felt about me perfectly clear yesterday. I'm surprised the sight of my naked body doesn't disgust you."

"Oh, Dimika," he started to say gently, but I interrupted him.

"No!" I screamed so loudly it echoed in the empty locker room. "Don't call me that. Never fucking call me that again. I'm not your Dimika. I'm not your mate, your lover, or even your friend. You have no right to call me that, Alexander."

I watched the emotions play across his face as I stood there panting in anger. My fists were clenched so tightly at my sides my hands started to hurt. Reaching behind me I shut off the water, then walked around him back towards my locker. I grabbed a towel along the way and started to dry off. Once at my locker I quickly dressed in clean clothes and pulled my sneakers back on.

I knew Alexander was still close, I could feel his eyes on me.

There had been a time when I would have loved for him to stand there and watch me dress. Not now, not anymore. Now it hurt to have him looking at me like that. Without a word I went back into the gym, dirty clothes in hand, to deal with the mess I had made.

When I got there I saw some of the warriors who worked in the infirmary working on the injured men. Everyone was still unconscious except Matteo. The look on his face told me just how pissed off he was. Yeah, I'd be pissed at me too. I sighed as I turned and headed over to him.

"Want to tell me what the fuck that was all about?" He asked, growling quietly at me.

"I'm sorry, Matteo," I answered kneeling in front of him. "I kind of snapped. I-I didn't mean to do that."

"Tell me this has nothing to do with the fact that Alexander was in the room watching?"

I turned my head away from his knowing eyes, unable to meet them. "I can't talk about that, Matteo."

"What did he do to you, Dimitri?" He asked gently, reaching out and touching my arm. I looked back at his face and saw he was no longer angry, but concerned. "You can tell me, Dimitri."

"I know. I just can't talk about it," I whispered, feeling my eyes burning again. No wonder Alexander didn't want to be with me, I cried like a baby all the time now. "When I can, Matteo, I'll come to you."

"Okay, Dimitri," he replied nodding, still looking worried. "I'll handle everything here, you just go walk it off, okay?"

"Are you hurt?" I asked looking him over. "I really didn't mean to injure everyone like that."

"I know, Dimitri," Matteo said, smiling. "Big bad-ass warrior just wiped the floor with six of his buddies. I'm fine, really. Just a dislocated shoulder from being tossed around like a doll."

"Jesus, Matteo, I really lost it," I replied, rubbing my hands over my face wearily.

"Don't worry about it, dude," Matteo chuckled. "We've all lost it at one time or another. It's all good. Just warn me the next time you want to play rough."

"Dirty, dirty, friend you are, Matteo," I snickered, knowing he had made the innuendo just to make me smile. "Thanks for handling all this for me. I think I just need to go lay down for a while."

"You do that, Dimitri," he replied patting me on the shoulder. "When you're ready to talk, I'll be here."

"Thanks." I stood and tried to collect my brains and

my self-control. While looking around the gym one more time at the chaos I had caused I locked eyes with Alexander. He was still watching me. Standing there in all his godliness, arms crossed over his chest, almost as if he was waiting for me to snap again.

Fuck him, and the horse he rode in on.

Chapter 3

Over the next week I did everything possible to avoid Alexander. It never fails; when I wanted him around and near me it seemed like I never got the chance, and as soon as I wanted him far away from me, he was everywhere. It was driving me crazy, and taking a major toll on my already shot nerves.

I didn't end up getting in trouble for my little demonstration. Everyone besides Alexander and Matteo thought I was truly showing my class the best moves to fight off a pack of Zakasacs, which ended up working out quite well. My class now looked at me with new respect and started training even harder. Glad my meltdown had a positive effect.

By the end of the week I finally gave up trying to keep to myself, and hiding. I decided to listen to Alexander's advice and try moving on from him. Not that I had any clue how to do that. But I had read once the best way to get over someone was to start dating another person. I didn't have time to date, they kept us really busy at the camp, so I thought of the next best thing, having sex with someone else.

I left my room in search of the two biggest sluts on the compound, Ben and Dean. They slept with just about anyone or anything they could get their hands on. I figured going to them was my best bet. My mental state wasn't strong enough to handle rejection right now, and I knew they'd never say no to me.

Sure enough, I found them in the lounge practically having sex already, with each other. They were infamous for their three-ways, but if they couldn't find another partner they had sex with each other, constantly.

"Well hello there, Dimitri," Ben purred when he lifted his head up from Dean's lips and saw me. "Are you just here to enjoy the show?"

His question threw me for a second. I hadn't expected them to be so forward. It took me a few tries, but I finally found my voice. "I'd prefer to join in, if you're offering?"

"We can always use another submissive for our pleasure," Dean said turning to look at me. He tilted his head as he looked over my body, "are you willing to be our little submissive, Dimitri?"

"Yes, I want to play," I answered, swallowing loudly. I felt sweat start to form on my back and my palms getting clammy. Was I about to make a big mistake?

"Then come here so we can see our new sub," Ben

replied hopping down from the pool table he had been sitting on. I took a deep breath and went to him. He reached out and touched the side of my face as he ran a hand over my chest. "Nice, very nice, Dimitri. What do you think, Dean? Will he play our games nicely?"

"Only one way to find out," Dean replied as he moved behind me and ran his hands over my back and ass. "Take off your shirt for us, little sub."

I nodded and pulled my shirt off over my head. I looked straight into Ben's eyes as their hands started to run over my now shirtless body.

"On your knees, bitch," Ben growled. At first I hesitated a second, not realizing he was talking to me. Dropping to my knees I was faced with Ben's hard cock. He had pulled it out when they watched me take off my shirt. Not sure what to do, I looked up at Ben. He had an almost feral smile on his face. "Good little sub, waiting until you're given permission before doing anything."

"Oh, he is going to be fun to play with," Dean purred as I felt him kneel behind me. "Suck his cock, sub. I want to see you deep throat Ben's hard-on."

I opened my mouth and slid my tongue over the head of dick in front of me. Never having given head before I was nervous I would do it wrong. The moan I heard from Ben told me I must have done something right.

Feeling more confident I leaned in and wrapped my lips around his cock, sucking it gently while running my tongue around the large mushroom head. Closing my eyes, I leaned forward, trying to get into the blow job I was giving.

"Prepare his ass, while I fuck his face," Ben hissed as I felt his hands in my hair. I was just about to pull back and ask what he meant, but he grabbed my head roughly and slammed his cock down my throat. Of course, never having sucked anyone's cock before, his sudden actions caused me to start choking. "Swallow it, bitch. Breath through your nose and suck my cock."

I listened to his advice and put my hands on his thighs to try and brace myself. He pulled out of my mouth a bit, barely giving me time to get adjusted, before he slammed his dick right back down my throat. I was temporarily distracted when I felt Dean's hands on me, pulling off my shorts. Ben picked up the pace of his thrusts into my mouth. I grabbed his hips and held him in place as I moved my head up and down on his cock.

"Don't hold me still, sub," Ben growled. "I want to fuck your face. That's a part of being a submissive, you take what we give you and ask for more. Beg for more."

I wasn't really sure that's what being a submissive was really about, but what did I know? I released my hold on his hips and let him thrust into my mouth, though I kept him from pushing in enough to choke me again. This was supposed to be about pleasure, not pain. Just then I felt Dean shove two lubed fingers into my ass. I knew I was too tight to have them start with two fingers, and the bite of pain made me gasp.

"Wait until you get back here, Ben," Dean said, sounding like a kid in a candy store. "He's so fucking tight. I want his ass."

"I get his ass, you can have his face. Hurry up and get his ass ready for me, he's too good at sucking cock," Ben groaned. "I won't last much longer at this rate."

"Fine, but next time I get his ass," Dean grumbled. I was startled how they both talked about me like I wasn't there. Especially considering one had his cock down my throat and the other had his fingers in my ass. Was this what sex was really like? It wasn't like I was expecting tender making love, but this wasn't what I wanted either.

I screamed around Ben's cock when Dean shoved a third finger in my ass and started wiggling them around to open me up. I was only on my knees, not on all fours, so the angle was tighter than if I was bent over. Ben seemed to get off on watching Dean causing me a little pain and started thrusting faster.

"He's ready, now move," Dean said as he pulled his fingers out from my ass. "I want to feel his hot mouth on my cock." Ben pulled out of my mouth with a loud pop, as he released his hold on my head. Dean moved in front of me and laid down on his back, legs spread. His groin was so close, if I leaned over I would have my face right on it. He gave me a wide grin, showing his fangs as he started stroking his cock.

"Bend over and suck him, sub," Ben said from behind me as he pushed me forward. When I was on all fours, Ben smacked my ass hard. It stung a bit, but it wasn't not pleasurable at the same time. What the fuck was that all about? As much as this wasn't going like I thought it would, it seemed I liked to be dominated and spanked. Well if that isn't fucking irony for you. I was probably the biggest warrior on the compound and the biggest pussy all at the same time.

I leaned over and sucked the head of Dean's cock into my mouth. He didn't grab my head like Ben, which I was grateful for. He was willing to let me explore on my own. I ran my tongue up and down his thick shaft, trying with all my heart to get into it. I was grateful they were both so wrapped up in their pleasure, neither seemed to notice my own dick had yet to get hard.

"I said suck his cock, bitch," Ben growled as he smacked my ass again. "Take his whole dick in your mouth like I made you do with mine."

The burning from where his hand slapped me was starting to turn into pleasure that radiated over my skin. I leaned down more and swallowed Dean's cock as far as I could. Once my nose hit Dean's skin I felt Ben spank my ass several more times and push my legs out wider.

"I think our little sub likes it when you spank him like a bad boy," Dean moaned. "Fuck him hard, Ben. I want to see if he goes to town on my cock. Or maybe he just likes to be spanked instead of fucked?"

I didn't have time to answer or even think of how I would have answered, because Ben grabbed one of my ass cheeks and roughly pulled them apart. He guided his dick into my hole, only pushing in a few inches at first.

"You were right, Dean, he's really fucking tight," Ben hissed. "This is going to be so much fun."

As I was still processing Ben's words he thrust forward hard and slammed his cock all the way into my ass. I cried out around Dean's dick as Ben dug his nails into my hips. Great, on top of everything else, Ben allowed his hands to shift into claws. That was going to leave marks.

"So fucking good and tight," Ben groaned as he started thrusting into me as hard and fast as he could. I would have had trouble catching my breath with just his fierce pace, but I also had a cock in my mouth. Focusing on what I was doing I tried to enjoy the dual sensations of sucking one cock while being fucked by another. Dean cried out, causing me to look up at his face while still blowing him.

But it wasn't Dean's gaze I caught, it was Alexander's. He was standing just outside the doorway in the shadows of the hall. My cock instantly swelled at seeing him watching me. I should have looked away from his eyes, I needed to look away from him. But I couldn't. Instead I sucked on the cock in my mouth even harder as I never broke eye contact with the man I wished I was sucking.

Ben's claws dug deeper into my hips, causing me to moan loudly. He took it as a sign of enjoyment and started thrusting into me even harder. While he didn't rub my sweet spot every time like Alexander did, I still found myself getting close to coming. I reached under myself to grab my hard cock.

"No, you don't get to come until we tell you, sub," Ben sneered as he leaned over and knocked my hand away from my dick. "If you're a good enough fuck, we'll let you come next time."

I wanted to get pissed off at the way they were treating me, but I had agreed to play their games. Instead I kept swallowing Dean's dick as hard as I could, my eyes never leaving Alexander. Ben started swatting my ass again, and I moaned loudly. That seemed to be all Dean needed to climax.

He stiffened under me an instant before his cock exploded in my mouth. It was already so deep in my throat it wasn't a matter of swallowing his cum down, just not choking on it.

"Yeah, that's it, bitch," Ben panted as he fucked me and spanked my ass at the same time. "Swallow all his yummy cum. Lick up every last drop of it like a good little sub."

Ben's own dirty words seemed to push him over the edge as well. I felt him give my ass a few last hard thrusts before he cried out and filled my ass with his seed. Dean's dick had softened and slipped out of my mouth as Ben collapsed against my back. Alexander still stood there, never taking his eyes off me as he adjusted himself in his shorts.

"Oh yes, we'll play with you again, Dimitri," Dean purred as he panted below me. "You're a very good sub for us."

I wanted to roll my eyes at him, instead I pushed off the ground and let Ben slide to the side of me on the floor. Once I was on my knees only again, I pulled back up my shorts and reached for my shirt. I finally turned away from Alexander's gaze, embarrassed now about what I had just done with the two of them.

"Next time, I might not want to be the sub," I said to both of the men on the floor as I pulled on my shirt. "I think next time one of you will be the sub."

"We don't play that way, Dimitri," Ben said, looking at me. "If you're not willing to be our sub, then you get nothing from us."

"So be it," I answered as I turned and walked out of the other door. There was no way I was going to be near Alexander after he stood there and watched our little show. Moving quickly I headed towards my room. It was hard, considering it was only my second time having sex and Ben had been really rough with me. I was sore and could feel Ben's cum trickling down and out of my ass while the blood he drew on my hips seeped into my shorts.

"Did you have fun being their whore, Dimitri?" Alexander asked when I came around the corner and almost crashed into him. I looked past him down the hall. Fuck! I was only several yards away from my room. Alexander's room wasn't even on this floor. He had deliberately tried to intercept me before I got back to the safety of my own room. The question was why?

"What do you care, Alexander? Just leave me alone," I said, trying to push past him. Instead he grabbed my arm and spun me so that my back slammed into the wall. Without thinking I cried out from the pain. After the fucking I just got, the last thing I needed was my ass banging into the wall.

"Why, Dimitri? Why did you let them treat you like that?" Alexander growled in my face. "They hurt you for god sakes! I can smell the blood and wounds on your hips."

"It's none of your fucking business," I snarled. I wanted to fight him so bad right then, but he was right. I was hurt and I wouldn't risk making it any worse. "At least they only hurt my body. You treated me way worse."

"I didn't hurt you," Alexander said. The tone of his voice had softened and he seemed almost confused. "I didn't treat you like a whore and bleed you."

"You did hurt me," I whispered, turning my head so I didn't have to see him.

"How, Dimitri? How did I hurt you?" Alexander asked, trying to turn my head back to look at him. But I wasn't having any of it, I couldn't look at him right then. I'd rather he snapped my neck than have to look into his gorgeous eyes. "I was not cruel or rough with you."

"That's a matter of opinion."

"I did not hurt you," Alexander said, starting to get pissed again. "I won't be compared to those assholes downstairs. I did not treat you as they did."

"No! You were worse," I snarled and pushed him

away from me. "You may not have been rough with me physically, but you broke my fucking heart! You shattered it!"

"Dimitri, I didn't mean to," he started to reply, but I cut him off.

"Why do you care, Alexander? You don't want me, you were clear enough about that," I yelled. "So what is it? Am I some game to you? You don't want me but you don't want anyone else to have me either? I'm not your fucking toy."

"That's not it at all," Alexander answered softly, reaching out to me again. I moved out of the way so he didn't touch me. The look on his face was one of pain. Why the fuck was he hurting? I should have kept my mouth shut and just walked away. It would have been the smart thing to do. But hell, I've never been accused of being smart.

"I wish you would have just killed me during the challenge," I said, taking a step back from him. "I'd rather be dead than living with this pain, this confusion. I wasn't the only one declaring I was yours when you fucked me, Alexander. You said I was yours too. Then you said you didn't want me, didn't care about me. It would have been kinder just to have killed me."

"Dimitri, don't say that," he gasped as he stepped towards me.

"It's the truth. I wish you had killed me," I replied before I turned and walked back to my room. I didn't even bother checking his expression or looking to see if he was following me. Instead I walked into my room and slammed the door behind me. I couldn't deal with him right now. I needed to be alone and lick my wounds, quite literally, considering my hips were still bleeding.

* * * *

The next night after dinner I headed back to my room to be alone. When I got there, I found a note on my door. I opened it up and read the message.

Dimitri,

I heard you played with Ben and Dean last night . . . that you were looking for a little sub of your own now. If you want me, I'm all yours big boy. Come to my room after dinner, I left the door open for you. I'll be naked and ready for your big cock to pound my ass!

Kisses,

Rune

I read the note at least five times before the words sank in. Even with my broken heart, I had thought it was a note from Alexander. How fucking stupid was that? Probably as stupid as I was pathetic.

Even more confusing, how had Rune heard about last night already? Living in the main house on the warrior camp was like living in a dorm the way everyone gossiped. I had always done what was needed to stay out of the gossip before. It never crossed my mind that last night would be so juicy everyone talked about it.

Could I really do this? Go fuck another warrior I barely knew? It had to be better than being on the receiving end of casual sex. After last night I knew I would never be involved in anything like what Ben and Dean did to me again.

I opened the door to my room, tossed my gear and the note on my bed. Glancing quickly in the mirror, I decided I was presentable enough. I took a deep breath and prepared myself to play someone else's master before leaving my room and jogging to Rune's.

Once I reached the door, I didn't bother knocking on it. I just opened it and walked right in. What I saw almost made me turn and book it out of there. Rune was spread eagle on the bed stroking himself.

"Oh, thank god, you came," he said excitedly. "I wasn't sure you would come, if I was too forward? But who knows, right? Some people like it when a man is forward with them, even if it's not typical submissive behavior . . ." Rune was talking so quickly I could hardly understand him.

"Shut up," I told him and he immediately closed his mouth and stopped playing with himself. He got up off the bed and fell to his knees in front of me.

"May I suck your cock, master?" He asked as he eyed my groin before looking back up to my face.

"No," I answered. Not because I didn't want to know what it felt like to get a blow job. It was more the fact I hadn't gotten hard yet. I didn't want Rune to realize the sight of him naked wasn't doing anything for me. "Go over to the desk, bend over it and spread your legs."

Rune's eyes went wide, and he smiled at me before jumping to his feet and doing exactly what I asked. Even though it was dark in the room I could see just fine with my vampiric sight. From across the room, looking at Rune from behind, I realized something. He was about the same height and build as Alexander. He also had black hair that he had pulled back into a loose ponytail. The instant I recognized the similarities and thought of Alexander I was hard.

"Are you ready for me?" I asked as I shed my clothes before walking up behind him.

"Yes, master, I've prepared myself for you," he replied quietly. Rune was shaking with anticipation. But in my mind, he wasn't Rune anymore, he was Alexander.

"Good," I said as I let my hands roam over his back

and ass. The shudder that went through him at just my touch made me rock hard. "Then I'm going to fuck you now. I'm going to fuck you so hard and so fast you'll be screaming in pleasure."

"Oh god," he moaned as a shudder went throughout his body. "Be rough with me, master. I want you to dominate me, take your pleasure from me."

"I will," I growled as I spread the cheeks of his ass and started to push my cock into his prepared hole.

"Fuck, you're huge," Alexander, I mean Rune, moaned. Then I thought, *fuck it. I could pretend he was Alexander. Like Rune would care anyways. He was getting what he wanted out of this.* "Yes, master, please, master. Give me more, master."

"You want more? Beg me."

"Please, please, *please*," Alexander moaned as I pushed myself into him. I thrust my hips forward and pushed the rest of the way in. Both of us moaned loudly when I bottomed out in his ass. "Hurt me, master. Fuck me until I bleed."

That snapped me out of my lust filled haze. Make him bleed? What the fuck did that mean? Man, it was just like I attracted all the crazies.

"Bleed from where?" I asked as I started working my cock in and out of him.

"I only prepared myself a little for you," he panted under me. "I like the pain of rough sex. I want it to hurt. I want you to fuck me so hard while I'm tight that you cause my ass to bleed. I'll be healed by tomorrow, but I like lots of pain with my sex."

"If that's what you want," I answered, shrugging my shoulders before grabbing his hips. I threw all my strength and weight behind my next thrust. The desk banged hard against the wall but I could barely hear it over Alexander's scream. I pounded into him with everything I had, loving the tight feeling wrapped around my cock. He had lubed himself up well, but I hadn't put any on my cock, so it was a rough ride for sure.

"Yes, oh yes, master," Alexander cried out in between thrusts. "Yes, it hurts so good. Harder, the desk is biting into my cock."

I kept up my ferocious pace, but turned my head so I could see what he was talking about. Sure enough, he was bent right over the edge of the desk, his cock smashed up towards his stomach over the corner. Ouch! That had to fucking hurt like a bitch. Well, it wasn't my dick there. Though I can't imagine the blisters and splinters he was going to have in his cock.

"I need more pain master," he grunted as I fucked him like an animal. "Hit me, pull my hair, hurt me, please."

"Shut up," I growled as I kept thrusting into him. While I wasn't going to judge him for the type of sex he wanted, the visual he was giving me was ruining the sex for me. I wasn't going to start beating on him while I fucked him, instead I moved one hand to his shoulder and the other to his hair. I pounded into him harder now that I had better leverage. I fisted his hair and pulled his head up roughly.

He screamed in pleasure as I heard some of his hair being ripped out from his scalp. I ignored it and kept thrusting into him. He started screaming out, "harder, harder," over and over again. Alexander stiffened under me before he cried out so loudly the walls shook. I felt the muscles in his ass clamp down on my cock. I assumed he had reached his climax, and him tightening like that around my cock pushed me over the edge.

I screamed in my head, *Alexander.* Then I gave his ass a few last thrusts as my cock exploded inside of him. The last thrust was so hard the desk broke. We landed in a heap on top of the broken desk, my dick still pulsing inside of him. When I stopped panting and my cock had softened I pulled out of him and stood up. It was only then I realized that it really had been Rune I had fucked, not Alexander.

Rune had passed out. I shook my head as I reached for my clothes and got dressed. What the fuck had I just done? Instead of thinking too hard on it, I went back and picked Rune up and put him on his bed. I would have been concerned if it wasn't for the big smile on his sleeping face. His chest and abs were cut up a little from the desk shattering, but other than that he looked okay.

I felt dirty. I was disgusted with myself and felt like the whore Alexander had called me. As tears started to form in my eyes I ran from Rune's room. I didn't stop running until I was back into my own room. Not bothering to clean myself up I crawled into my bed and pulled the covers up over my head. Then I let the tears fall. I lay there, curled up in a ball on my side, and sobbed. I cried for what I had just done, what I did the night before, and the regret in my heart that it still hadn't helped me forget Alexander.

Chapter 4

The next morning I still felt about the same about life and my feelings for Alexander. I had really hoped to have a change of heart to enjoy with the afterglow of sex. But at least I wasn't teaching the early morning class for the pre-transitions today. Instead I rolled out of bed later than normal and headed for the mess hall. Once there I loaded up my tray and found Matteo.

"How are you feeling?" I asked, wary that he'd let me join him.

"Dude, you've got to let it go already," Matteo replied rolling his eyes. "I told you the next day I was fine, Dimitri. I had a bump on my head and a dislocated shoulder, no big deal, man. I've had a lot worse."

"I'm glad you're okay," I said quietly as I started shoveling food into my mouth. "I felt really bad about it."

"Well stop, Dimitri, there's nothing to feel bad about," he snickered. He got quiet all of a sudden, causing me to look up from my food and see what he was looking at. Matteo was watching Rune give me lover's eyes from across the room. "Dimitri, please tell me you didn't sleep with Rune?"

"Do you want me to lie?" I asked glancing away from Rune. I hadn't even noticed he was in the mess hall with everyone. I also couldn't believe the man was giving me goggly eyes after last night. What kind of man wants more of the treatment I gave him last night? I left him passed out and bleeding after fucking him so hard I broke his desk.

"Dimitri, Rune's into some weird ass shit, man," Matteo said carefully. Now I knew he was really worried about me, sarcastic Matteo wasn't known for his careful approach to a situation. "I mean, it's not my business who you hook up with, but I'm your friend. I'm worried about you, Dimitri. I know something happened after you challenged Alexander. I also know you think you managed to hide from everyone that you love him, but I'm your best friend. I know."

At first I felt bad for worrying Matteo, but the more he talked, I started to get pissed off. It wasn't any of his business and I didn't have to answer to him. "Yeah, great, you figured out my big secret, Matteo. But I'm not the only one hiding who I'm in love with, am I? I'd be careful where you throw stones, buddy."

"I'm not throwing stones, Dimitri," he replied sighing. "I've known for a while that you knew about my feelings for Nate. I'm just saying I understand what it's like to love someone you can't have. I know what you're going through and I want to help if you would just let me."

"You have no idea what I'm dealing with," I hissed at him as I slammed my glass down on the table hard enough for it to shake. "Nate would be with you in a blink of an eye if you'd just pull your head out of your ass. Alexander doesn't love me, he doesn't want me, okay? Is that what you wanted to hear? Or is it that he keeps playing with my feelings and watching me," I continued, trying to hold the tears at bay. "During the sex it was all, *you're mine forever, Dimika.* As soon as it was over he said he didn't love me, didn't want me and to move on. But every time I'm trying to move on, it's like he's there watching me, playing with my heart."

"Oh, god, Dimitri," he whispered, looking lost as to what to say next. It took a few moments before he continued, "I know Alexander cares. I don't understand why he's doing . . ."

"Yeah, great, thanks for the pep talk," I said, interrupting him. There was no way I could sit here right now and listen to this shit. Alexander didn't care, he just liked to fuck around with my heart to boost his ego. "This was fun, but I'd really rather be pulling my fingernails out one by one than having this talk."

I stood and took my tray over to the dishes area. Yeah, I had been a prick to my friend, but seriously? I mean, seriously? He thinks lying and telling me that Alexander cared for me would help? Right before I was about to turn around, I felt a hand slide over my ass.

"Will you come and play with me again tonight, master?" Rune whispered in my ear as he pressed himself up against me. "I'll beg or do anything you want for sex that awesome again, master."

"Don't touch me without permission, sub," I hissed turning my head to the side but not quite looking at him. He immediately stopped touching me and took a step back.

"I'm sorry, master," Rune replied quietly. "I suppose you have to punish me now."

The tone of his voice told me he was anything but sorry. He sounded like he was shaking with excitement at the prospect of me punishing him. I decided to try playing with him again, but this time on my terms.

"I want you ready for me right after dinner," I said quietly so that no one could hear us. "You are to be prepared for me. I want your hands tied up over your head, facing the wall, back turned towards the door. Do I make myself clear?"

"Yes, master," he replied, his voice full of lust. "I will be patiently waiting your arrival."

"Good, now leave me," I answered as I scraped my plate into the garbage. When I finally turned around, Rune was gone. I was in charge of the training schedule for the pre-transition warriors and I had scheduled myself to lead their morning exercise today. This meant I had to get my ass over to the obstacle courses right now.

Jogging over there I ignored the whispers and glances I was getting from the other warriors. Honestly, I always thought I would mind being part of the latest gossip, but I just couldn't bring myself to care. Instead I was ready to give my trainees one of the hardest workouts of their lives.

"Alright, that's enough talk," I said loudly to the group when I got close enough. The chit-chatting stopped instantly. "We're splitting into two groups today and heading over obstacle course C, there and back. At the sound of the whistle, I want one hundred push-ups, two hundred sit-ups, and fifty chin-ups. The same will be repeated at the halfway point and the finish line."

It took me everything I had not to burst out laughing at all the jaws hanging open. The course I selected was a six mile trek over hell. And to make them run it twice . . . well I knew it was mean, but there was a purpose to this torture.

"I'm sorry, Dimitri," my buddy Yuri said quietly,

coming over towards me. He was about as good of a friend to me as Matteo. I normally had one or the other of them to help me as trainer with my classes. "Did you just say course C, there and back?"

"Yes, I did," I said to him but loud enough so everyone could hear me. "How many of you are less than six months away from turning twenty-five?"

About half the class' hands went up. Pre-transition vampires from warrior families came to training camps based all around the world the day after their twenty-fourth birthday. Since every vampire hit their transition midnight of their twenty-fifth birthday this gave them a year to prepare and learn a good foundation for being a warrior before their bodies caught up to them.

"Alright, those that have less than six months are with me," I instructed. "Those with more than six months are with Yuri."

"If that's what you want, Dimitri," Yuri said quietly, studying my face carefully. "Are you sure this has nothing to do with recent events?"

"Yes, I'm sure," I snarled in his face. "I've had this on my training schedule for months, Yuri. You have a problem with my tactics, or think you can do better, I'm ready to accept your challenge."

"I'm not challenging you, Dimitri," Yuri replied

holding his hands out in front of him and a gesture of surrender. "I'm just checking on the program, that's all."

"You done checking?" I asked sarcastically.

"Yeah, I'm done," he answered as he turned to go back towards the second group.

"I want ten minutes between the groups," I said, ignoring the interruption with Yuri. "In theory, my group should be faster anyways. But if you've never run this course before, pair up with another in your group who has."

I waited as everyone got situated and ready. When the time came, I blew the whistle and dropped to do my push-ups along with my class. After which I did my sit-ups and pull-ups as well. I wasn't surprised when I was done before most of them even started their sit-ups. Pre-transitions were much stronger than a twenty-four year old human, but they weren't even in the same league as trained warriors.

There was a reason I wanted their arms to stay tired before and during the course. That many push- and pull-ups should have most of them feeling as if their arms were gelatin. The course started with a three story rock climbing wall to climb up and then rappel down on the other side. I had been watching the class rely way too much on their upper body strength to maneuver through most of the courses.

The proper way was to split between upper and lower body strength during the courses. No matter how many times I corrected them, I still caught them doing it wrong. Now that their arms were exhausted, they would have to rely more on their lower bodies to complete the course.

"Use your legs more," I yelled as I watched the first few start on the wall. "Climbing isn't all about using your arms. Push up with your legs to reach the next handle."

I almost laughed when I saw the light bulb go off over Yuri's head as I was instructing. He understood the method to my madness now. I twisted and gave him a smirk, in turn he gave me a full smile and shook his head. I wasn't a fan of explaining myself and I was glad he'd caught on. While I wouldn't give in and clarify my actions to Yuri, especially in front of the class, I also didn't want him to think I was letting my emotions run me.

Nate, my best student, was the first up and over the wall. He led the group to the next part. Climbing the ten foot ladder wasn't the hard part. It was crawling along the hundred foot rope upside down. Again, most of the class had been pulling with their arms and using their legs to balance. Now, with their arms tired, they had to use their abs and back to push themselves along and bring their legs back up towards them.

The goal was to teach them alternative ways to handle any situation. Right now it was just how to run the course with tired arms. But out in the field it could be how to escape with a torn shoulder or ligament. Not to mention if your back was clawed up. Zakasac claws had a type of poison in them. I could speak from experience when I said it felt like acid was being poured into the wound.

Once the first of them were almost caught up with me and done with the rope I led the short run to the over-and-unders. That's what we called the different sizes of logs that were held up on stilts. Basically, you'd jump over the first one, drop to the ground, and roll under the next. Then you'd get back up and repeat the process. It wasn't as simple as hopping a fence that came to your chest.

The logs were thicker for one thing, and there were over a dozen of each height. It was the back and forth that made them so hard to complete.

Next were the ropes. There was a hundred yard mud hole with a platform on either side. You had to hit the first platform at a run and jump to the first rope. The momentum would take you to the next rope that you had to grab on with one hand before letting go of the first rope. Again, the force of the swing would cause you to propel to the next rope, and so on.

The main trick was timing. If you didn't hit the

platform at a fast enough run when you grabbed the first rope, you wouldn't be able to reach the second rope. Also, if you didn't grab the second rope at the right moment while letting go of the first, you wouldn't be moving forward. The second ropes original position would cause you to swing backwards if you didn't go of the first rope in time. Plus, these weren't the small, hang your laundry up type of ropes. Each rope was at least twenty feet long and probably a good seventy-five pounds each. If you timed everything out right, it was an advantage, if not . . . well, your ass landed in the mud.

Once you were past the ropes you came to a few vampire-made hills of dirt and rocks. While everyone saw on the way up that you couldn't run full force and sprint up them, it was actually on the way down that most people got tangled up. Especially the younger trainees. I've watched hundreds of trainees over the years try to run down the hill like you would run on flat land. The result being that they end up rolling down the hill head over ass. While amusing, it had the potential for many injuries.

After that was a crawl through the dirt. There were side by side ditches several hundred yards long. On top of them were heavy logs wrapped with barbed wire. It worked on a pre-trans' ability to handle enclosed spaces and move into position without making a target of themselves.

Lastly, there were several incline walls. Like the over-and-unders you had to use some upper body strength to lift yourself up, but you also had to push up with your legs to clear the top of the wall. The goal was to practice rolling and sliding down the wall while still being able to spring right back to your feet. Helpful training if you're ever under fire and you need to dive and roll out of the way.

One by one my part of the class finished up and started on the next set of sit-, push-, and pull-up's. Like before, I made sure to do my own while they did theirs. When the last of them were finally at the pull-up part, the second half of the class was starting to finish up the course. I sat there and smiled as Yuri was barking at his group to get their ass in gear. It was one of the reasons I always chose him or Matteo to assist me in training.

I wasn't one for yelling to motivate. While I understood the concept, and how it worked for lots of the trainees, it just wasn't my style. Mostly because when I was the one in training there wasn't anything anyone could have said to or yelled at me that would have made me move faster. I was my own worst enemy in that only I could push myself harder. I didn't care what others thought of me or my abilities, it was a matter of proving it to myself.

Once the second group wrapped up the course my

group was ready to head back. I led the way at a leisure pace so they could keep up with me. Even then it was definitely a work out for them. On the other side I finished the rest of the drill and then watched as my group finished. I made sure to pay attention to those who did it all the way through, and the ones who cut out part of the instructions and said they were done.

Honor was something warriors take seriously. The ones who were cutting corners didn't have any and I would be addressing that shortly.

By the time the class completed it the whole exercise had taken a little over two and a half hours. I had scheduled three for the training so I made sure Yuri took the time to lead them through lots of stretching to help them recover. Once that was over I had to bite my lip to keep from laughing at the amount of hate-stares my class directed at me. They would thank me one day. As I had my instructors when I realized how much their training had helped me be the warrior I am today.

* * * *

I was late to dinner that night, not really wanting to stay and hang out much. Quickly loading my tray and sitting in the corner I caught Rune's eye as he got up to leave. He had the same goggly eyes focused on me and a knowing smile. I watched as he left his tray by the dishes area and scurried out of the mess hall.

"You had them run course C twice with extra workouts thrown in?" Matteo asked with a raised eyebrow as he appeared in front of me. "Yuri told me it was quite the show."

"What of it, Matteo?" I asked, instantly on the defensive. I took my training schedule very seriously, just as I did my role as head of the pre-transitions.

"When he first told me, I thought you had fallen off your rocker," he said, shaking his head as he sat down across from me. "But then he told me how the class did. Also he figured out why you threw in the extra calisthenics."

"Get to it, Matteo," I grumbled in between bites of food. "The foreplay is getting tiresome."

"Fine, I'm trying to pay you a compliment you bastard," Matteo snickered. "All of us thought you were nuts when we heard what you did. But Yuri was there and he was impressed."

"You didn't think they would be able to do the course twice and the workout, did you?"

"No, I would never have bet they could," he shook his head again.

"How much do you want to bet none of them thought they could do it either?" I asked, raising my eyebrow. His head snapped up and his eyes widened.

"You did this so they would see how far they've come in the training, didn't you?"

"And here I thought you were just a pretty face," I snickered, then shoveled some more food in my mouth. "Yeah, I wanted to show them how far they really can push themselves. Partially so the ones about to hit their transition believe that they are strong enough to survive it. The other part was so they can see all the different training coming together and what it accomplishes."

"Smart, Dimitri," Alexander said from behind me, making me jump.

"Thanks, Alexander," I said, trying to hide my reaction to his voice and his body being so close to me. "Next I want to start something I read about from the human military. We start it next week."

"What is it?" Matteo asked curiously, leaning forward on his elbows.

"In the United States Navy they have a competition at all the different training bases," I said before swallowing some of my drink. My throat was suddenly dry now that Alexander was listening. "It's called The Brigades. Any trainee can fight, and it's like a big boxing tournament.

There's no prize at the end, besides being named number one. I think it will be a good way for our young men to be able to learn some honor."

"So, are we going to let them box, or use swords?" Matteo asked, eyes wide again. "Because they're not supposed to learn how to use swords until after their transition."

"No swords," I answered, loving how excited he was getting. It matched my own enthusiasm and helped me ignore the fact Alexander was still listening to the conversation. "But not straight boxing either. We teach them a combination of mixed martial arts and that's what the tournament will be. Everyone who wants to participate will work for one month during their free time with the warrior they ask to sponsor them."

"In other words getting them to train longer and harder, but as if it was their own idea," Alexander said, moving to the side so we could both see him. "Quite impressive, Dimitri."

"Uh, thanks," I said, looking down, suddenly not hungry anymore, for food that is. I also had the problem of a major hard-on now. "I've gotta go, I have a date."

"A date? Or are you going to fuck Rune again?" Alexander asked watching me carefully.

"Didn't know you were so into the latest gossip,

Alexander," I answered, not looking at him. While it wasn't an answer to what he asked, it was the best he was going to fucking get from me. "Catch you later, Matteo."

"Later, man," Matteo replied, looking between me and Alexander. I ignored the gazes of both men as I got up and headed towards the dish area. Was it chicken shit of me to leave right then? Oh fuck yeah. Personally, I looked at it as bowing out gracefully before it got any worse. At least that was my story and I was sticking to it.

Once I was outside Rune's room, I didn't bother knocking, just turned the knob and walked in.

"Master, is that you?" He asked in a voice that just about purred.

"Shut up, you're only allowed to moan, groan, scream, and cry, nothing else," I ordered as I closed the door behind me. I figured out last time that the more he spoke the more he ruined my fantasy of it being Alexander. And right now, my cock was hard and throbbing after seeing the man. I wasn't going to let Rune talk and ruin it. Especially when he looked just like Alexander with his back to me right now.

Rune simply nodded as I stalked towards him. I didn't stop until I was fully pressed against him and he could feel my hard dick pushing into his ass.

"My cock is hard for you, the idea of being inside

your ass and fucking you silly gets me this hard," I hissed as I pushed my hips forward. He groaned as a shiver went throughout his body. Rune, had asked me to punish him, torture him. Tonight I was pissed off and frustrated with Alexander, and Rune was going to be my fill-in. I closed my eyes and licked along the side of his neck. From that instant on, he was Alexander to me again.

Alexander whimpered as I kept licking along his neck and shoulders while I moved my hands to grab his hips. His hands were tied over his head as I had ordered. The rope was hung over a hook, his body flush against the wall. I ran my hands over his hipbones towards the center of him, stopping just short of touching his cock. Instead I pulled one hand back and quickly slapped him hard on the ass.

His cry of pleasure told me I didn't have to start off slow. He was enjoying this amount of rough play right off the bat. With the mood I was in it was fine with me. I leaned back just enough to pull my shirt off. Then I leaned forward again, pushing my chest into his back and rubbing my hands all over his chest. I ended up moving right over his nipples and pinched them.

"You like that, don't you? This is supposed to be me punishing you," I hissed after he moaned in ecstasy. My answer was to pull on his nipples even harder. He squirmed against the wall and cried out. I gave him a short break, long enough for me to pull off my shorts and shoes. Then I went back to torturing him.

"Master . . ." he moaned and I dug my fingers into his shoulders.

"Not one fucking word, or I walk out that door," I growled. Alexander nodded his head so fast a part of me was shocked it didn't fall off. I let my fangs scrape alongside his neck and he cried out in pleasure. Reaching around Alexander's body I yanked his cock hard as I let my right hand slap his ass with all I had. I started to worry I was being too rough, but his moans of pleasure told me otherwise.

Deciding to take it up a notch I let my hands shift into claws. I ran them up the front of his thighs, hips, and abs. Not enough to draw blood, but there were going to be some serious scratches and marks later. In a flash I switched positions so that my claws were roughly pulling the cheeks of Alexander's ass apart.

"You're all ready for me, very good," I hissed as I sank my fangs into his shoulder. I had to be careful not to drink, since that's how we mated, but the bite was still very pleasurable for Alexander. He started thrashing against the wall, thrusting his hips until they slammed against the wood of the wall.

I ripped the butt plug out of his ass, lined up my hard cock, and slammed all the way into him. We both moaned as I bottomed out. Pulling my fangs from his neck, I grabbed his hips harshly. I let my claws sink into the flesh there as I started pounding furiously into his ass.

"So fucking good," I grunted in between thrusts. "I'm going to fuck you so good, you'll never want another cock in your ass."

He must have liked what I was doing and saying because he was screaming as he pushed his hips back to meet me. I knew it was going to be another rough ride. Alexander might have prepared himself and used lube, but I didn't before I started fucking him. I let my right claw slip off of his hip and move to his hard cock.

"Oh, you like that, don't you my little slut?" I asked as he moaned loudly. I wasn't just jacking him off while I fucked him, I was scratching my claws along his dick as well. "Is that what you are, my little pain slut?"

His only response was to scream when I used a little more claw. I looked down over his shoulder as I pounded into him, there was a little blood running out of his cock now. I had the same reaction any vampire would to the sight and smell of blood during sex. I started fucking him harder. Really, I was surprised I even had it in me. We had started out hard and fast and now I was pounding into him at almost a brutal pace.

"God!" I cried out, "So fucking close. I'm going to shoot my load into your ass soon. I know that's what you want."

Alexander started to whimper. I was about to ask him if I was playing too rough, but then he stiffened up and shot his cum all over my hand and the wall. His muscles clamped down on my cock. That was all I needed to push me over the edge. I roared out my release and thrust into his ass a few more times.

"Tomorrow night I want you on all fours with your hands tied to the headboard," I told him a few minutes later after my heart stopped racing. I pulled out of his ass, causing us both to groan. Looking down at my cock, I realized I was still hard and ready to go again. "But for now, I've still got a hard cock."

I made a snap decision then. Reaching up I took his tied hands off the hook. I ruined part of the fantasy when I spun him around and could see he was Rune again.

"Get on your knees and suck my cock, you whore," I growled. Rune's eyes got wide in surprise, but then he grinned wide. Without a word, he dropped to his knees. His hands still tied in front of him, he simply opened his mouth. I guided my dick into his waiting mouth and he immediately took me all the way down his throat. "Fuck, that's good."

I grabbed a handful of the hair on the back of his head and shoved him on my cock harder. Rune didn't even gag. Seems someone had a lot of experience sucking cock. I looked up at the ceiling and closed my eyes. His throat muscles were like heaven around my dick. He kept swallowing over and over again as I pushed his head down on me. Then he started humming.

All sanity left me when he did that. I grabbed his head with both of my hands, already having shifted my claws back. I thrust my hips hard into his face, much like I had pounded into his ass. And he took it and kept humming. It was fan-fucking-tastic. I didn't last long this time, screaming as I came. He swallowed every drop of my cum before pulling back.

My now soft cock left his mouth with a loud pop. Still staring at the ceiling, I stood there for a while panting. I had locked my knees so I didn't collapse but still it was a thought. Instead I took a step back and grabbed my clothes. I turned away from Rune as I got dressed.

"Remember what I said about tomorrow," I said over my shoulder before opening the door and leaving. Wow! I couldn't believe I had come like that twice in a row. When I reached my room I didn't bother undressing, or even pulling back the covers. I simply landed on the bed face down and passed out.

Chapter 5

The next week I spent my days working and training the pre-transitions. At night, I would go to Rune's room and fuck him like a madman. Was it the best thing for me to be doing? Probably not. But it was great stress relief. But I always made sure he was facing away from me so I could keep pretending it was Alexander.

About an hour after breakfast, Matteo came racing into my office at the training facility.

"Dimitri," he said, panting, obviously trying to catch his breath.

"What's up, Matteo?" I was starting to get worried. My best friend looked completely freaked out.

"It's Alexander," Matteo answered after he finally calmed down. "He was on a routine escort mission for the head of the council. They were hit by a nest of Zakasacs. The others were able to get the councilman to safety but Alexander stayed behind to give them a head start."

"Is he?" I asked my throat closing up. I couldn't even get the rest of the question out. My hands hurt and I looked down to see I was clutching my desk so hard I left an imprint.

"No, they went back after the councilman was secured," he answered, his face showing concern. "They took him. The Zakasacs took Alexander with them. The warriors couldn't find him or any trace he was killed. They found his sword. He would never leave his sword, Dimitri."

I was out the door before he even finished. Matteo was already running alongside me as he finished explaining about the warriors finding Alexander's sword. He was right though, Alexander would *never* have left his sword for any reason. They must have gotten him unconscious and taken him with them. Either they had some trick up their sleeve or Alexander was going to become their dinner.

Only two things were keeping me sane as we raced to the main house. One, you couldn't be turned into Zakasac unless you killed. Alexander would rather have died than have that happen. Two, he was still alive. The man I loved was taken by a nest of Zakasac and I had no time to think of anything but getting him back.

I hit the door to the main house so hard it went flying off its hinges and across the hallway. Not even slowing down, I headed to the war room. It's where we had most of our surveillance and intelligence equipment. Normally we plan missions, and sometimes escorts, like the one Alexander had been on.

"What do we know?" I asked as I barreled into the room. Of course I got five different responses, all at the same time. "Shut up!" I yelled loudly enough for it to echo. Everyone immediately closed their mouths.

"Show of hands, who was there?" I asked, three hands went up. One of them was Yuri, I would trust his report more than anyone else's. "Yuri, talk to me."

"It was supposed to be a simple escort," Yuri stated. "Alexander, me, and the two others, escorting the head of the council. They hit us about a half an hour before dawn. Alexander told us to get the councilman out of there and he would meet us at the emergency rendezvous point. We stashed the councilman, waited about twenty minutes, and went back to the attack site when Alexander didn't show."

"You found no body?" I asked. I know Matteo had told me, but I needed to hear it from someone who had been there.

"No, Dimitri," Yuri answered shaking his head. "We found three dead Zakasac, blood, and obvious signs of fighting. We also found Alexander's sword, but no Alexander. I just checked with one of the warriors we left at the emergency rendezvous point, he still hasn't gotten there. When we couldn't find him we high tailed it back here to recoup and come up with a plan."

"If they hit you that close to sun-rise, their lair has

to be close," I said, thinking hard. Zakasac were what human legends of vampires stemmed from. Sunlight burnt them to ash. "How far away from here was the attack."

"Not even half an hour," Yuri said, his eyes going wide as he realized what I was getting at. "You don't think . . ."

"I don't know, but if you wanted to get into this facility, taking one of us would be their best course of action," I snapped. "I want this place on lock down. Everyone to the main house, even the pre-trans. Evan, Drake, you guys were on the escort mission, right?"

"Yes, Dimitri," Drake replied, while Evan just nodded.

"Fine, you're in charge of weapons," I barked out. It wasn't that I was pissed, it was just a time when I needed to show I wasn't fucking around and they would listen to me right now, without question. Also, I was the second warrior in charge on this camp. With Alexander gone, it was left up to me. "I want every pre-tran armed with hollowcase bullets. Get Nate to help you do a head count and make sure no one is missing, got it?"

"Loud and clear, boss," Evan said just before they turned and raced out the doors. I knew they would get the job done. After everything that had happened, leaving a warrior behind, they would need to feel useful this second, be kept busy. Even if they didn't normally handle the pre-trans class they still knew lockdown procedures and what to do.

"Matteo, I want you to handle the rest of the lockdown procedure," I continued. "I want everyone here and accounted for, like, five minutes ago. We still have hours before sundown, but I'm not taking any chances. I want the lasers armed as soon as we have everyone in here and accounted for."

"You got it. Can I make a suggestion?" Matteo asked.

"What?" I asked raising an eyebrow. I was ready for him to give me shit about my feelings for Alexander clouding my judgment.

"We've got enough gear for all the warriors and the pre-trans to have coms," Matteo said, holding his hands out in front of him. "I think right now all of us should have our mission earpieces in. That way we're all connected and no one can get surprised."

"Good idea," I answered nodding. "Rune, you're on that. You're our techie guy, so we need you for the rescue op, but get one of your guys you trust to do it."

"I'm on it," he answered heading over to the other side of the room. It still surprised me at times, that as submissive as he was in bed and with sex, Rune was our head tech guy. And he was the best of the best at it.

"Yuri," I said, turning to him. "I want everything from escort mission. I want to know who the fuck knew about it. And I also want you to plot out on the digital maps what happened where."

"All over it," Yuri replied nodding at me before turning away.

Once everyone was running around following my orders, I sat at the conference table and went over the list of warriors at the camp. Of the forty warriors, I split us into two groups. I chose the best warriors for the first group, which would be coming with me on the rescue mission. The second group was going to stay here and guard the fort. Quite literally, but actually the camp, since it really wasn't a fort.

The camp was out in the middle of fucking nowhere, east Wyoming. There was a reason that this location was chosen. It gave us necessary privacy from humans of course, but we would also notice if any enemies got too close. The convoy with the councilman was hit about a half an hour away from here. And with another half an hour before sun-rise I had me a general area of where their lair could be. Worst case for the camp, they could be right next door. Best case for the camp, but maybe worse case for Alexander, they could be almost an hour away.

I finally looked down at my watch. It was almost noon. Given it was summertime the sun wouldn't be setting for almost another eight hours. Fuck! That still wasn't as much time as I would have liked. Right now the Zakasac would be dead to the world. Some of the older, more powerful ones could get up before nightfall, but even they had to stay protected.

The closer we got to nightfall though, the more likely Alexander would become someone's snack. I pushed the morbid thought out of my head. I couldn't think about him dying and also do my best to get him back here.

"Nate says we got all the pre-trans," Evan said as he came back into the war room. "They're armed to the teeth and in the mess hall. Drake and I figured that would give them at least something to do since it's lunchtime."

"Good plan," I answered nodding, then handed him one of the lists I'd made up. "You and Drake are in charge when I leave, Evan. We'll keep you in the loop on coms but I need you here to keep them safe. It's a smart plan for the Zakasac to try and take out warriors before they become warriors."

"I agree," Evan said as he looked over the list. "These are the twenty you're leaving with us?"

"Yeah, I also want you to talk with Nate," I explained. "The pre-trans who have been here less than six months are just cannon fodder, but the ones who are closer to their transitions are excellent marksmen. Set it up so they are protecting the cannon fodder in case there is an attack and Zakasacs are able to break through your lines."

"You got it, Dimitri," he said as he slapped me on the shoulder. "Bring Alexander back. It didn't feel right to leave him behind. We want him back."

"If it takes my last breath, he'll be home before nightfall, Evan," I replied.

"That's why you're the man in charge," Evan said with a smirk before he left the room.

"Alright, everyone is inside the main house," Matteo said, coming up behind me. "Is that who's going?"

"You got it," I answered without even looking back at him. I handed the list to him over my shoulder, "Get those twenty set up and ready to head out in fifteen minutes. And I want the tracking dogs."

While vampires had a great sense of smell, nothing was better than well trained tracking dogs. They were able to separate smells and stay on task better than anything else in the world. Every camp always had a pack of at least ten well trained dogs for search and rescue ops.

"Who's in charge while we're gone?" Matteo asked, pausing before he walked away.

"I've got Evan and Drake," I answered looking at

him.

"Good choice," he replied smiling before he walked off.

After that it was a matter of getting everyone into their positions and knowing their assignments. Fifteen minutes later, we were loaded and out the door. I watched everyone get their gear and the dogs loaded into the SUV's as I leaned against the first car with Yuri.

"We'll get him back, Dimitri," he said quietly.

"Of course we will," I replied scrunching my eyebrows and looking at him.

"Look, Dimitri, I know . . ."

"Don't, Yuri," I said, backing away from him. "I can't deal with that now. Right now I'm just the warrior in charge of a rescue op, nothing else. If I think of anything else I won't be able to focus."

"Okay Dimitri," he replied as he headed to the driver's side. I had decided he would lead the convoy since he knew best where the attack happened.

Minutes later, everyone was loaded and I was climbing into the passenger's seat. Once we were through the main gates I contacted Drake to secure all the entrances and turn on the lasers. Those lasers were actually Alexander's idea. They were ultraviolet lights woven into a very tight weave. Any Zakasac that tried to cross them would light up like fireworks and be instantly dead.

I was so deep in thought about the plan, getting Alexander out alive, and no one else getting hurt, that we arrived where the convoy got hit before I realized we'd even gotten close. We all jumped out of the SUV's and started evaluating what we saw. I hadn't even taken three steps when I felt that familiar tingle up my spine. I calmly took a few steps in each direction, trying to see which way made the feeling get stronger.

"Matteo, forget the dogs," I yelled as I pulled my sword out of the sheath strapped to my back. I barely had time to meet my best friend's eyes before I started off in the direction the feeling was coming from.

All vampires had heightened senses, extreme healing capabilities, and strength. We warriors also all had one special gift, something we were born with, and the gifts differed greatly.

Mine was being able to tell when there were Zakasacs close. I got a feeling that went up my spine like a vibration. It could be compared to the way the hair on your arms and neck rises when you know there's danger around you. But for me, it was more exact. Every one of the warriors knew it was my gift and so they didn't even question why I raced off. They just followed. The stronger the feeling got, the faster I ran. If Zakasacs were close,

Alexander was close.

After a few miles of full-out sprinting I saw where I was heading. It looked like an old, abandoned hunting cabin. I figured it was a place the Zakasacs would hold up because all the windows were boarded up. No sunlight coming in.

"Two and three hit the sides," I hissed into my com-piece as we got closer. I had split the twenty of us into four teams of five. "Four take the back, one, we go in the front. Get there now."

I saw different teams keep up the pace to go around the cabin and in front of us. My team slowed it down so we could go in and have the other teams hit the building right after. Matteo, Dean, Shane, and Kevin were right behind me as I burst through the front door. What I saw had me seeing red, literally.

There were three Zakasacs drinking from Alexander. Without even thinking, I rushed them. One swing of my sword decapitated two of them. They had been drinking from Alexander's wrists, kneeling in front of him. Both had stopped drinking to look up when we busted through the door, so I had a clear shot at their heads without a chance of hurting Alexander.

The third one jumped towards me. I let him impale himself on my sword and then raised it towards the ceiling.

He was down in two pieces before I knelt in front of Alexander. I heard some fighting going on around me, but none of that mattered, only him.

"Alexander, it's Dimitri," I said as I put my sword away and cradled his face in my hands. "Talk to me Alexander."

"Dimika? Is that really you?" He asked me quietly while he smiled widely. "I knew you would come for me, Dimika."

"MEDIC!" I turned my head and screamed, "I need a fucking medic here!"

"I'm okay, Dimika. Just tired, so very tired," Alexander said softly as he tried to raise a hand to touch my hands on his face. The effort it took was evident, he didn't have the strength to do it. "Just hold me my love, my Dimika."

"No, don't sleep. Fight, goddamn you!" I said loudly, slapping his cheek to keep him aware. I pulled him against my body and hugged him fiercely. "Don't leave me Alexander, please, stay with me, I love you. You can't leave me like this. MEDIC!"

"Dimitri, let him go," someone said, but I could barely hear them. I was holding onto Alexander, trying to will him to live. I was rocking us back and forth as the tears poured down my face. "Dimitri, it's Sam, let him go. I need to look at him."

"Sam?" I asked confused before turning to look at him. Then it hit me, Sam was a medic. Immediately I released Alexander into Sam's arms. I backed up out of the way so the other medics could get to him.

"Alright, let's get him loaded up," Sam said as two of them picked Alexander up. I followed them blindly outside and saw someone had gone back to grab one of the SUV's while I was freaking out. "Dimitri, hop in and hold him steady."

I nodded at Sam and climbed into the back seat. They handed me Alexander and I grabbed him under the shoulders and pulled him into the back seat with me. Sam climbed in after us so that Alexander was in the middle. He was busy trying to put an IV into Alexander but I was too focused on keeping him awake.

"Look at me, baby," I cooed trying to stay calm. "Alexander, stay with me, okay?"

"I'm always with you, Dimika," he answered as he tried to arch up and kiss me. Alexander wasn't strong enough right now and I had no problem leaning over and gently touching my lips to his. "That was better than what I've dreamed of."

"You can have as many kisses as you want, whenever you want, Alexander," I whispered, still crying.

"Just don't leave me. I need you."

"As I need you," Alexander replied as he started to pass out.

"I gave him something to sleep, Dimitri," Sam said, having seen my concern. "I've got blood running into him, replenishing his supply. But he doesn't need to be awake for the drive back. Those bites have to hurt like a son of a bitch."

"When are we . . ." I started to ask, but realized the SUV was already moving at top speed. I looked up front and saw Matteo was driving like we had hundreds of Zakasacs on our ass. I had been so focused on Alexander I missed my friends taking over and getting us the fuck home. Well, that's what friends are for I guess. Turning back to Alexander, I ran my hand down his face lovingly. He was safe. He was alive. Nothing else mattered, anything else we could work out.

* * * *

"Dimitri, what are you doing here?" I heard someone ask. I rubbed my hands over my eyes, and then sat up like a shot.

"Alexander, you're awake," I said, moving towards him. I had fallen asleep in the chair next to his bed in the clinic. Everyone had kept telling me he was fine, and I could leave. But I couldn't. I had to stay until I knew he was going to be okay.

"Yes, I'm fine, Dimitri," he replied rolling his eyes. "What are you doing here?"

"Making sure you were okay," I answered, starting to get confused. "They said you were going to be okay, but I wanted to be here when you woke up."

"Why?" Alexander asked raising an eyebrow. And that one word told me so much.

"You don't remember what you said to me after we rescued you, do you?"

"I was suffering from several Zakasac bites, and major blood loss," Alexander replied smirking. "I'm sure I said some wondrous things. What? Did I tell you I loved you or something stupid?"

"No, of course not," I answered, feeling cold. I had dropped the hand that was reaching out to touch him down to my side. "I'm glad you're better."

I turned and ran from the room.

"Dimitri . . ." Matteo said as he tried to grab my arm as I went past him in the hallway. I ducked out of his reach and just shook my head. I couldn't talk right then, it hurt too much.

Now I knew the truth.

No matter how much I wanted Alexander, he would never love me, want me. And all the trying to get over him in the world wasn't going to erase the fact I loved him, no matter how many times he hurt me.

Chapter 6

The next few days I kept completely to myself. I went to teach my pre-transitions but other than that I stayed in my room and refused to open the door. I didn't eat or sleep. Also, I didn't go see Rune. While he might not have minded me using him like that, I did. I didn't want him, I wanted Alexander. And that was never going to happen so I resigned myself to a life alone.

I was getting lots of stares and whispering about the Zakasacs I killed. Everyone was so impressed I killed three of them before any other warriors had gotten in the door. It had taken several of them to kill the other two that were there. I missed that part of the mission by being so focused on Alexander. And I really didn't give a shit I had impressed people. I'd done it without thinking because I saw them hurting the man I loved.

The sweep team that stayed behind when I left to help tend to Alexander had found the motherlode. There were detailed plans of kidnapping one of the warriors from each camp all over the world. The enemy was getting organized and banding together, something we had never seen before. Zakasacs were more solitary creatures, once in a while living in small groups. But even those normally contained no more than three or four members.

The plans and details that were found showed dozens upon dozens of them grouping together, all for the same goal. To wipe out the vampire councils and every warrior they could get their hands one. Even the ones that hadn't hit their transition yet.

Reports were still coming in from other warrior camps and councils about the damage already done. And for them to have organized a worldwide attack to this magnitude . . . we weren't dealing with the Zakasacs of old. This was a whole new breed of enemy. One with leadership and goals extending beyond just death and destruction.

Alexander had been interviewed by the council once he recovered. He ended up learning from the Zakasacs and giving away nothing they wanted to know. Not only had the council been thoroughly impressed, it seemed to feed his legendary status.

The fourth day after my talk with Alexander in the clinic I got a note from Matteo. He had some questions about the training schedule and really needed to talk to me. I knew it was more than that, he probably wanted to check if I had lost my mind yet. But either way I wasn't just going to ignore him.

"I don't know what you're talking about," I heard Alexander growl as I walked up to Matteo's office in the training facility.

"Don't lie to me, Alexander," Matteo replied. "You know what my gift is."

"We're not allowed to use our gifts on each other," Alexander sneered. "Besides, you're still wrong, you just don't know how to use your gift."

"Bull fucking shit, Alexander!" Matteo yelled. "And I can't turn off my gift. I see people's auras. Every time anyone lies to me, they light up like a fucking Christmas tree. You love him! Why can't you just admit that to yourself and him? You could be happy. Dimitri would do anything for you, why deny you love him?"

"Enough," I screamed as I walked into the room.

"Dimitri, I was just . . ." Matteo started to say.

"Just what, Matteo?" I growled, "Trying to trick Alexander into admitting he loves me when you asked me to come here right now? So what, your grand scheme failed. He doesn't love me, fuck, I don't even think he likes me as a person. I didn't ask for your help, I don't want your help, Matteo. Just stay the fuck out of it and leave it alone. He doesn't want me, I'll eventually find someone who does!"

I didn't bother to wait for anyone to answer, I just

turned and stormed out the office. I got as far as halfway down the hallway before I felt a hand grab my shoulder. It spun me around and I was all ready to yell at Matteo some more. But it wasn't Matteo, it was Alexander. And instead of yelling . . . I gasped as he pushed me hard against the wall, and kissed me.

His lips were just as supple as I remembered. It wasn't any soft peck this time. Instead it was demanding and full of heat. Alexander pushed his body against mine as he wrapped his arms around my waist. I gladly yielded to the kiss. I felt his tongue running along my lips, telling me to open up for him. His tongue felt like heaven in my mouth. My arms found their way around his neck, pulling him even closer to me. I loved the way the line of his body felt against mine. I melted when I realized his cock was hard and pressed into my thigh. Was his dick really hard for me? Just from kissing me?

"I can't fight it anymore," Alexander hissed against my lips as he reached into my shorts and started stroking my cock. "I can't watch you be with another, Dimika. You're mine."

"Yes, oh god, yes, Alexander," I moaned as he stroked me faster. I turned into a lust-filled pile of goo when he started licking along my jaw.

"Say it, Dimika," he growled in my ear. "Admit you

are mine and that you will never touch another man."

"I'm yours, Alexander," I hissed as he nibbled on my ear. It seemed I really liked that. Between Alexander playing with my dick, feeling his hard cock pressed against my leg, and him biting on my ear I was overwhelmed with sensations. I felt my balls tighten up as my climax started to come. I screamed out my release, "I love you, Alexander."

I had just started coming all over his hand as he sank his fangs into my neck. It sent my cock into overload, exploding as my knees gave. Alexander held me up as he drank from my neck. My brain couldn't even process what was happening.

"No!" He raised his head, screaming, and let me go. I fell to the floor in a heap and watched Alexander go down on all fours and throw up. He threw up my blood, and kept throwing up. "I can undo this."

"Don't bother, Alexander, I'm already dead," I said as I scrambled to my feet.

"No, Dimitri," he said, holding out a hand to me, but then turned away to vomit some more. I started to back away down the hall on shaky legs. I couldn't watch this. The idea of being mated to me was so horrible to Alexander he was making himself throw up my blood before the mating tie fell into place.

I kept walking backwards until I hit the side door

that led outside. I hit the bar, turned, and ran. At first I was half running, half limping until my legs felt more solid. By the time I made it to the main gate at the camp I was running at a full sprint.

Alexander didn't want me, he just didn't want me to have anyone else either. Why did he hate me that much? What had I done to deserve this torture?

"Dimitri, come back, let me explain," Alexander said in my head. Guess that answers the question on whether the mating bond would take or not. Well that was a waste of my blood. I couldn't answer him though, even if I had wanted to. Technically, he had mated with me. I hadn't bitten, or mated with him. So he could talk in my head but I couldn't respond in his.

It was a new, disorienting feeling for me, hearing someone else's voice in my head. The day a vampire got mated was supposed to be one of the happiest of their lives. Instead I was running away from him knowing it would kill me but not caring.

After a vampire mates they have to mate and be bitten by their mate on a regular basis. I never really understood the science of it, something about our genetic makeup. Once you were bitten and mated, you needed your mate's fangs, the compound they gave off, to stay alive. It was the same compound in our saliva that helped wounds heal, but when mated our bodies start craving it. Now that he had mated me Alexander's bite was as important to my health as food and blood were.

I didn't care. I wanted to die right then. How could I live knowing Alexander had just mated me and it was so horrible to him, he tried to stop it? Why had he even bitten me in the first place?

"Please, Dimika, come back to me. I have to explain to you. Don't run away from me to your death," he said in my head. If I hadn't known better, I would have guessed that Alexander sounded scared. What did he have to be scared about? I was the one who was going to die.

"Shut up!" I screamed out loud at no one, knowing it didn't make a difference. "Just shut the fuck up and get out of my head!"

By then I was already miles away from the camp, no one was around me to hear my screaming. Not that I would care if everyone heard me and thought I had lost my mind. I had. Alexander finally cracked me.

Did crazy people know they were crazy?

That thought caused me to finally stop running and laugh. And I knew it wasn't a good laugh. I laughed like a loon as tears streamed down my face. Falling to my knees I started to slam my fists down into the ground, all the while still laughing and crying. Yep, I had lost my mind.

Unfortunately there weren't any asylums for crazy vampires. We went crazy and the council sent warriors to kill us.

That left me with two choices: death by warrior because I'd lost my marbles, or a slow death because Alexander wasn't biting me on a regular basis, one that would feel as if I was starving to death. Geeze, gotta love these options!

* * * *

I had been wandering for a couple of days before I finally collapsed from exhaustion. I was pretty sure I was still heading in the original direction I started in. But then again, I was so out of my mind I was surprised I wasn't seeing dancing pink elephants. Not to whine, but I was tired from two days straight of walking or running, thirsty from lack of blood between the normal need to drink and what Alexander had taken from me, and starving for food.

Not to mention the fact I was ready to shoot myself in the head just to stop hearing Alexander's voice running through my mind. Added to all that, my muscles were weakening from the need to feel my mate's bite and the chemical it sent into my body.

Alexander was constantly talking to me in my head,

but he never said what I needed to hear to turn around and go home. Oh sure, I could tell he was concerned for me. But he never said those three little words . . . *I love you.* So I still was choosing death over living an empty life where he was my mate. A mate who didn't love or want me.

It wasn't until I started seeing things that I really started to worry. There I sat on the ground, leaning against a tree, talking to Alexander's voice in my head, when I saw him. It wasn't just Alexander, it was Matteo, and a few other of my friends as well.

"Over here," Matteo yelled as he raced towards me. "Dimitri, can you hear me?"

"You're not real," I replied as he got close to me. I tried to push him away but I was too weak. He felt solid and real. I wanted to believe my best friend was really there but I knew in my heart it was just my mind playing more games on me.

Alexander knelt in front of me, taking my face in his hands. "Dimika, are you alright?"

"No, I'm not alright," I sobbed trying to pull away from my Alexander mirage. "You don't love me, you hate that you mated me. Hell, you're not even really fucking here. You talk, talk, talk in my head and I just want to chop it off. I hate you for what you've done to me! You torture and tease me, not wanting me, but not wanting me to be with anyone else. You've pushed me until I've turned into the pathetic, blubbering mess before you."

"I know Dimitri," Alexander replied nodding as tears flowed down his cheeks. "I know you can never forgive me, and I will never forgive myself. But I won't let you die either, so you will just have to add this to list of my sins."

"What . . ?" I started to ask, tilting my head to the side to look at him, and that's when he struck. He was lightening quick, sinking his fangs into the side of my exposed neck. My moan was actually half in protest, I wanted to be left alone to die and not have to feel the pain of his rejection anymore. The other half of my moan was sheer ecstasy. My cock swelled and exploded seconds later, giving me one of the strongest orgasms of my life just from his bite.

I watched dazed as Alexander pulled away from me and sat back on his heels. We never stopped looking at each other, even as Matteo reached in between us and slapped a bag of blood onto my fangs. He moved my hands so that I was grasping the bag but I was too weak to hold it up to my mouth. Alexander quickly caught one of my hands in his, helping me keep the blood to my mouth. His other hand started stroking my hair as he whispered to me in Russian.

Once the first bag of blood was emptied, Matteo

switched it out for a second, then a third. By the time I was done drinking I'd stopped counting how many bags of blood I'd drunk. I had that too full feeling, like when you drink too much water and almost feel it swishing around in your stomach.

Alexander stood and lifted me into his arms like I weighed nothing. It was impressive since I weighed much more than him and was inches taller as well.

"This is real, isn't it?" I asked searching his face.

Alexander only nodded, still looking pained at my appearance.

"Then put me down," I said as harshly as I could. "I don't ever want you to touch me ever again."

"No," he answered shaking his head. "I won't, I like the feel of you in my arms. And I put you in this condition so I will reverse it. Plus I will have to bite you every few days for you to live, Dimika. And you will live."

I started crying again, my entire body shivering in his arms. "I don't want to live, just let me die."

"No!" he growled fiercely as he moved towards the SUV I hadn't even noticed. He lifted me in and got me settled on the seat as if I was a small child.

"I hate you," I repeated in between my bouts of crying.

"I know, Dimika."

"Stop calling me that," I wailed. "It hurts too much to hear it."

He searched my face for a few moments before nodding. "As you wish, Dimitri, but I still won't leave you to die."

"You can't make me live, Alexander."

An almost evil grin came across his face, "you'd be surprised what I can make someone do."

"Fine, I concede you can make me live," I replied, still trying to get away from him. "But even you can't make me want to live."

"I will spend the rest of my long, long life trying to change that," he said gently, reaching out to touch my face. His arm dropped to his side when I flinched away from him.

"Yeah, and I'm sure you'll change your mind about that in a few more minutes," Matteo grumbled from the front seat of the SUV. "Hurting my friend even more and causing as much pain as destruction in your wake."

Both of us turned and looked at Matteo, speechless.

He ignored us and started the car.

I took his lead and ignored Alexander, leaning against the side of the seat and window. Closing my eyes I cursed that this was really happening. I didn't think any version of heaven or hell would pick up where my life left off and just continue from there.

Chapter 7

I woke up chained down to a bed in the clinic. Like anyone would, upon realizing I was trapped my initial reaction was to struggle. I tried for several minutes, finally giving up and turning my head when I heard the door open.

"I wanted to be here when you woke up," Alexander said, moving towards my bed. "I'm sorry I was late. And don't bother struggling against the chains, you won't be able to get out."

"Why am I chained down?" I growled, still trying to reach for him even though I knew I couldn't.

"They'll be there until we know for sure you won't be a danger to yourself," he replied, reaching out to touch me.

I turned and tried to bite his hand, but he moved out of the way too quickly. "I'm not trying to hurt you, Dimitri."

"I don't want you to touch me, touching me hurts."

"Not physically," Alexander said, shaking his head. "My touch doesn't bring you pain."

"It hurts my heart," I replied, turning away from him when the tears started running down my face. "Just leave me alone."

"I can't, Dimitri. You are my mate."

"No, I'm not," I grumbled still not looking at him. "Mates are wanted, mates are loved. Mates don't throw up the blood of the person they bite to try and undo being mates."

"I didn't do that because I didn't want you," Alexander replied as he touched my head. I closed my eyes, loving the feel of him touching me. No matter how much I hated him right then, I still loved him. Nice and confusing for me. "I did it because I didn't want you to get stuck being tied to me."

"What? That makes no fucking sense!"

"You deserve a better mate than I could ever be," he said quietly, still running his fingers through my hair. "I don't know how to be softer, loving, or even how to be close to someone. I never have. It was selfish of me to bind you. I've never wanted anything or anyone as much as I want you Dimitri. I always have. And it was so easy to ignore when I didn't know you felt the same . . ."

"Just stop it, Alexander!" Matteo yelled as he came into the room. "Leave him alone. Haven't you done enough?"

"Matteo, it's fine," I said, turning to look at him.

"No, it's not okay. I'm tired of watching him put you

through the ringer. He's might as well just beat the shit out of you every time he opens his mouth, it'd probably be less painful for you."

"This is not your concern, Matteo," Alexander growled.

"The fuck it isn't," he snarled back. "Here's how this is going to go; you don't talk to Dimitri unless he seeks you out. Every other day you will meet us in my office and bite Dimitri so this mating doesn't hurt him. Or so help me god, Alexander, I will kill you. And I'm not talking a fair, challenged death. I mean a kill-you-in-your-sleep evil revenge death."

"Only because you know you cannot best me in a real challenge."

"No shit," Matteo snickered. "That's why I'm threatening to kill you in your sleep."

"There's no honor in you," Alexander snarled.

"Not when it comes to my friends. I won't let you keep hurting him, no matter if it costs me my honor in the process."

"Enough," I screamed, getting both of them to turn and look at me. "I like Matteo's plan, but no more threatening each other."

Alexander's jaw just about hit the floor, but after a few moments he recovered. "If that is what you wish,

Dimitri. I will see you tomorrow after classes in Matteo's office."

"Fine, see you then," I replied and rolled back over away from him. "For now, please just leave me with my friend."

"He's gone," Matteo said a minute later. "It's going to be okay."

I started crying when he came and sat on the bed and put his arms around me. "No, it's really not going to be alright. I've been mated to a man who doesn't want me, doesn't love me, and is stuck with me for eternity."

"He does love you, I can see it in his aura. Alexander is just a dipshit when it comes to showing his feelings."

"Yeah, whatever, Matteo."

"Look, I want to get you out of those chains," Matteo said quietly. "But you have to promise no more trying to kill yourself."

"I didn't try to kill myself . . ." I muttered feebly.

"Running off knowing you were going to die is pretty much the same damn thing. You know I'm right and you're just splitting hairs."

"Fine, you're right," I replied grudgingly. "I won't kill myself and I'll let Alexander bite me so I stay alive."

"Good," Matteo said, raising an eyebrow and

searching my face. After a minute or so of examination whatever he saw seemed to pacify him. He started unlocking and pulling the chains off of me.

"Thank god," I groaned after they were finally off. "Can I just go lay in my own bed and get some sleep?"

"Yeah, Dimitri, you're not a prisoner," Matteo said as he helped me stand. "That was Alexander's idea. I trust you and if you say you're done trying to kill yourself, I believe you."

"Thanks, man," I replied, giving him a half hug once he got me out of bed. I kept my arm around his shoulders, because while I had refueled my blood supply and Alexander had bitten me, I still hadn't eaten anything in days.

As we made our way to my room I tried to ignore the stares from other people. I'm sure the rumors of what happened were running rapid. Warriors just don't leave the camp. I couldn't even remember a single instance when someone had just gone AWOL. Even more rare, warriors being mated to each other. Vampires weren't necessarily known for being homophobic, it was more that warriors put in their time of service and *then* looked for their mates.

When we got to my room there was already food waiting for me. It smelled great. Matteo helped me eat and get cleaned up. About an hour later I was full, clean, and tucked into bed. My head hit the pillow and I was out like a light. I didn't even hear Matteo leave.

*

I was having the best dream ever. Someone was stroking my cock and kissing my neck. I shivered from the dual pleasurable sensations and let out a moan.

"That's it, Dimitri," Alexander whispered in my ear. "Just enjoy it, my mate."

"No . . . what?" I asked snapping open my eyes and turning to look into Alexander's eyes. This was so not a dream. I reached down and grabbed the wrist of the hand playing with my cock. "Let me go."

"I just wanted to . . ."

"I don't fucking care," I hissed, as he let go of my dick. Once he did, I moved my grip up towards his upper arm. In one swift movement I launched him across my room. I was out of bed and on him before he could even sit up. By the time I realized I was doing it, I was punching in my mate's face.

As quickly as I started, I stopped. Scurrying away from Alexander and his now bloodied face, I sat on the floor, pulled my knees to my chest, and started to shake.

"I'm sorry, I'm so sorry," I sobbed over and over

between the tears and cries coming out of me.

"I deserved all of it and so much more," Alexander replied as he crawled towards me. I knew his face was already starting to heal since vampire cells regenerated wicked quick.

"I asked you to leave me alone, Matteo told you to leave me alone. Why can't you respect my wishes? Even after everything that's happened, you can't give me some time? I woke up to you playing with my cock. You know I don't want you touching me. Anywhere."

"I was just trying to show you that I do want you," he said sadly. I finally glanced up at him and he looked really distraught. "I thought if I could show you how I truly feel, you wouldn't be so upset. Or reject my advances any longer."

"All you showed me is you don't care enough to respect my wishes," I answered, starting to cry again. "And being attracted to me, or showing you want to hook up, isn't the same as me knowing you love me and really want me as your mate."

"How do I show you that?"

"I can't give you that answer," I said, shaking my head and moving away from him as he got closer. "Even if I knew what the answer was, it's something you have to figure out for yourself."

"You now understand why I tried to sever the mating bond before it started? I don't know how to be with someone. Love doesn't really conquer all, Dimitri."

"I don't know how to either," I answered running my fingers along my temples as the headache started to form there. "But I know better than to disregard the other person's wishes. You shattered whatever trust I had in you. I don't even believe you want me for more than a good fuck, let alone as a mate for life. Where we go from here, Alexander, I haven't a fucking clue."

"I am sorry, Dimitri," he said as he started to stand. He tried to hide it, but I saw the tear running down his cheek as he headed towards the door.

"You're always sorry, Alexander. But it never really fixes anything does it?"

"No, it doesn't seem to," he replied as he left, closing the door gently behind him. I just sat there for a while, watching the now closed door as if I was going to find the answers there.

It took a while before I snapped out of my daze. I looked at the clock and realized I had to get my ass in gear to get to class. In a flash I was dressed and out the door, jogging over to the gym. Once there I opened the door and walked in the gym, nodding to the other instructors. Of course, Matteo and Yuri were there, even if they weren't scheduled to be. I gave them a rare full smile so they knew I appreciated the back-up today.

"Is he still allowed to teach after cracking up and running away?" I heard one of the students ask in a mock whisper. Without even having to look, I knew it was Lance. He would be the only one stupid, and bold, enough to pull that kind of shit.

"My personal life has nothing to do with my teaching," I calmly answered him, making sure he had the full weight of my stare. "And it really is none of my student's fucking business, now is it Lance?"

"I would say that's up for debate," he snickered looking at his friends as if he just made the best joke ever. Twit. "I mean, now that you've cracked up, how can we trust you to really teach us what we need to know?"

"It's not for you to question . . ." Yuri started to answer, but I held up a hand for silence. I might be emotionally fragile right now, but I was still strong enough to handle Lance.

"Thanks, Yuri, but I got this," I said, smirking before turning back to Lance. "Since you're so concerned Lance, come on down here and I'll show you why."

"What are you going to do?" Lance asked suddenly paling.

"Answer your questions," I replied innocently.

"Now your instructor told you to get down here, so move your fucking ass."

"Yeah, we know how much you like ass, don't we?" Lance snickered as he started to make his way down the bleachers. Before I could even respond, Alexander was lifting the pre-trans off the floor by his neck. Fuck! I hadn't even seen him in the gym.

"Alexander, let him go, I've got this," I shouted to no avail.

"You don't ever talk to a warrior like that, ever," Alexander snarled in Lance's face. "That is my mate you are talking to, and even if you won't respect your instructors, I won't allow a little shit like you to talk to him that way. Do I make myself perfectly fucking clear?"

"Even you can't touch me," Lance sneered back. "You know who my parents are. That makes me un-fucking-touchable."

"You are not your parents. No one here gives a rat's ass who your parents are," Alexander growled. "We all come from warrior or council member families . . ."

"Dimitri doesn't," Lance smirked as if he had been waiting for the chance to throw that at me. "He doesn't come from nobility or warriors. He comes from nothing."

Alexander's retort shocked me down to my very core, "And yet look how far he's come? He's not even a century old and already number two at one of the best warrior camps in the country, maybe even the world." He paused as if waiting for his words to sink in, then still holding Lance up with his hand around the boy's neck, he turned to talk to the rest of the class.

"Being a warrior isn't about your roots, it's about who you are as a person. The moment you left your parents and walked through the gates, you became your own man. We are here to give you the tools to become great warriors, great men. What you choose to do with the instruction we give you is up to you. It's your choice. You can be like Nate, who's at the top of his class and already has warriors lined up to have him on their detail after his transition, or you can be like Lance and laugh at your teachers and show you have no honor."

"I have honor," Lance spat at Alexander.

"Is that so?" I asked raising an eyebrow as I moved closer towards him, trying to shake off the effect Alexander's words had on me. "Then why did you cheat last week when we ran through course C? You skimmed off some of your sit-up, pull-ups, and push-ups every step of the way."

"You have no proof of that!"

"He doesn't need to, he has another witness," Matteo answered Lance as he moved to stand next to me. "I saw it as well. Recent events have postponed our reprimand of your actions, but I think now is the perfect time to address it. Don't you, Dimitri?"

"I do," I said, trying not to laugh at Lance's distraught face. "And since you and Alexander seem to get along so well, I think your punishment should be a few days in his solo training. That is, if you have the time to give some one-on-one time to Lance, Alexander?"

Alexander turned to me with that evil grin on his face, "It would be my pleasure, Dimitri." He looked back at Lance, having wiped the look off his face and turned it back to his normal stone-faced demeanor. "Go change into your fatigues, boots and all, Lance."

Lance lost all his cockiness as Alexander set him down to his feet. Lowering his head, he headed towards the locker room without another word.

"For the rest of you," I said loudly, addressing the class. "If there are no other objections, you'll be running course B with Matteo and Yuri."

"No, Sir," they shouted loudly, all smiling. It seemed Lance getting his just dues had made a few of their days as well. They filed out to the locker rooms in silence, with Matteo and Yuri nodding to me before following them. Which left Alexander and I alone in the gym with only a few other instructors. As we stared at each other intently they seemed to get the hint and made themselves scarce.

I walked over to Alexander and he seemed to think I was coming to yell at him.

"Dimitri, I'm sorry. I didn't even realize what I was doing until I already had my hand around the boy's neck. I know you are more than capable of handling your own fights, it's just I couldn't let him stand there and disparage you."

Instead of yelling, I wrapped my hand around the back of his neck and pulled him towards me. I took advantage of his surprised gasp and slid my tongue into his mouth. The kiss was hot, filled with every conflicted emotion we must both have been feeling. I felt his hands moved over my waist, taking a moment to massage me there, before moving to my ass. Mine went around his neck until there was nothing between us.

We both moaned and leaned into the kiss even more. After a few more moments I finally pulled away enough to speak. "That was a good first step to winning back my trust, Alexander."

"That's not why I did it," he replied, his voice low and husky as we both panted and caught our breath. "I wasn't really thinking when I did it. I just knew I couldn't just stand there and let that little shit talk about you like that."

"I know that's not why you did it," I said gently as I leaned in for another quick kiss. "And that's why it meant so much to me."

"I care for you, Dimitri," Alexander stated, looking up towards my face and searching my eyes. I wasn't sure what he was looking for, a sign of my forgiveness maybe?

"Maybe I'm starting to believe that," I answered as I went to let him go.

"Please, not yet," he whispered. The look on his face was so full of need. I didn't want to let him go just yet either. "I've wanted to hold you for so long, I'm afraid this will be my only chance."

"I don't know either way," I replied, taking a deep breath before I continued. "I can't just forgive you, but what you did, what you said, helped mend my broken heart. But it's far from fixed, you get that, right?"

"Yes, I understand," Alexander said, nodding. "May I kiss you some more and then bite you?"

"No, I can't."

"Which part can't you do, Dimitri?"

"The combo," I answered starting to shake. "I can handle either another kiss, or you biting me. But both together is too intimate for me right now. I-I . . . it makes me . . . well, it's just . . ."

"Okay. It's okay," he soothed as he put his hand over my mouth. "I can't say I understand, but you're shaking. And that's not how I want you to be when I touch you like this. I promise to try not to push, Dimitri. I will give you the time you need."

"Thank you," I whispered as I kissed his hand over my lips. When he pulled his hand away, I leaned down and pressed my lips back on his. It wasn't as long a kiss as before, but it was almost more intimate. It didn't have the same heat, instead it was tender, loving.

"I will still see you in Matteo's office later today, right?" He asked when we broke the kiss and moved away from each other.

I simply nodded, unable to speak just yet after what we shared. Taking another few steps back I turned to head to my office.

"Dimitri?" He asked and I turned back towards him. "When the time is right, and you are ready . . . I do want you to bite me. I want us to truly be mates in every sense of the word."

I can't even imagine the picture I made right then. I'm sure my jaw hit the floor. Nodding, with my mouth hanging open, was the only acknowledgment I could give him right then. He smiled a little and then moved to leave the gym.

I stood there, still in shock, and watched him leave. He wanted me to bite him? Wow. As the thought began to sink in I realized my knees were shaking. I sat down on the bleachers before I fell on my ass. Turning the events over in my head I finally smiled. I had given up on the idea of living happily ever after, but maybe it hadn't given up on me?

Standing and heading to my office, I realized I hadn't asked Alexander what he had been doing in the gym in the first place. I got my answer when I opened the door to my office and saw the florist shop that was now in there. There were flowers everywhere. All different types, in many different arrangements, all in vases. On my desk was a small, white card. Opening it up I read the message.

I didn't know what type of flower you liked, so I decided to get every type there was so that I didn't miss your favorite. I am sorry for all the pain I caused you, but I cannot be sorry that you are my mate.

-Alexander

Again my jaw just about hit the floor, and I sank down slowly into my desk chair. I must have sat there for at least an hour, just looking around my office at all the gorgeous flowers he had gotten me.

Chapter 8

We met in Matteo's office right before dinner. Part of me wanted privacy for the intimate act of Alexander biting me. But the rational part of me knew we needed Matteo there as a buffer.

Matteo found me in my office hours before, still staring at my flowers. He seemed to have the same reaction I did. Though he got a big grin on his face after I handed him the card and he read it.

"Are you ready for this?" Matteo asked gently, snapping me back to the present.

"No."

"I'm sorry, but you still have to do it."

I nodded before speaking, "I know. I don't want to die, but you know what this will do to me. It's hard right now, knowing how vulnerable I'm going to be in front of him."

"It affects me just as much," Alexander said quietly from behind me. I didn't even turn around, but I definitely made sure Matteo understood how pissed I was at him. I can only image the look on my face because Matteo seemed to be having a hard time not laughing.

"Does it?" I asked, still not turning around to face Alexander, not even once I had calmed down.

"Yes. To bite my mate and not be able to touch him the way I want to rips my heart out of my chest. Not to mention I have to leave you to take care of the hard-on you give me."

"I can't believe you just said that in front of Matteo," I gasped, finally moving in my chair so I could see him. "Why would you put yourself out there like that?"

"Because I do not want any more lies between us," Alexander said, staring at the ground. "I lied to you for so long. I lied every time I said I didn't want you or love you. Now you are giving me the chance to work at being real mates. I won't risk it by telling anymore lies."

"Good," I said in a shaky voice. "I'm glad you're taking this seriously. I won't give you another chance, Alexander."

"I know that. I don't even deserve the chance you're giving me now."

"No you don't," Matteo grumbled under his breath. Both of us turned to look at him. I wasn't sure what Alexander's face looked like but I knew mine wasn't all that friendly.

"How do you want to do this?" Alexander asked, causing my focus to turn back to him. "Do you want me to lean over and just bite you from behind while you are sitting?"

"I think that would be okay," I answered, not having thought that far ahead. His suggestion did seem like the least intimate way to share a mating bite. "You can touch me though, I mean for balance or whatever."

I didn't so much see as feel him move in behind me and the chair. Alexander being that close to me sent a shiver through my body. He put his hand on my left shoulder as he started to lean down towards my right. I felt his breath on my neck and I started shaking with anticipation.

"You want this as much as I do," he whispered before kissing my neck.

"Yes," I hissed as my eyes rolled into the back of my head. I cried out Alexander's name as his fangs sank into my neck. As before, my cock instantly swelled and at his first pull from my neck my dick exploded. "Oh fuck, yes!"

The hand Alexander had on my shoulder slowly moved down and across my chest possessively. I noticed the gesture while having my mind altering orgasm. My whole body practically convulsed as he drank from me.

Alexander finally pulled his fangs from my neck and licked the wound. "I'm sorry I took so much, I could not help myself."

"I-I- it-it's okay," I stuttered out as he started to pull away from me. Everything in me screamed to pull him closer but I knew it was better this way. Suddenly Alexander moved to kneel in front of me, between my legs, bracing his hands on my thighs.

"Bite me," he hissed as he tilted his head to offer me his neck. "Make me yours as you are mine."

"I-I can't." I quickly closed my eyes against the tears. "We can't. I can't complete this until I know you really will stay this time."

"I've always been here, Dimitri," he said as his hands moved up my legs.

"Stop this Alexander," Matteo growled and I heard him move from his chair. "You're pushing him too hard."

"And that's the last thing I wanted," Alexander sighed and pulled away from me. I opened my eyes then and saw he had sat back on his heels and removed his hands from me. "I will learn to control myself better, Dimitri. I am trying, it's just being near you, drinking your blood, weakens all my best intentions."

"Okay," I answered, still shaking. "I guess I can understand that."

"Do you really?"

"Yes, I get it," I snarled, now getting pissed off. "I

feel the same way, except then my head reminds me of all the pain and hurt you've caused. And that helps me keep my senses."

"I'm never going to be able to make this up to you, am I?" Alexander asked as he got to his feet. The look on his face was less than friendly.

"I don't know," I answered quietly. "But that's not my fault."

"No, it's not," he replied, looking sad. Without another word he walked to the door and let himself out.

I stared at the door, finally letting the tears fall, until Matteo came over and hugged me. That's when I started crying out loud instead of just in my heart.

* * * *

Two days passed and Alexander and I met in Matteo's office again where he bit me. This time it seemed almost to hurt him to bite me. I wasn't sure why, but the last thing I wanted was to cause Alexander pain. This wasn't some type of warped and twisted revenge thing, it was more a matter of my survival until I was sure Alexander was serious about being with me as a true mate.

That night as I prepared for bed I made a somewhat rash decision. Instead of getting into my bed I found myself standing outside Alexander's room. I must have raised my hand at least a dozen times to knock as I stood there. I jumped when the door opened.

"I didn't mean to scare you, but I could smell you through the door," Alexander said, looking confused. "I figured if I left it until you knocked, by the time you decided if you were or not we might have missed sleeping tonight."

"Yeah, sorry, I kept rethinking the wisdom of doing this."

"Doing what, Dimitri?"

"Coming here to sleep with you," I answered, and quickly continued when I heard his gasp. "I mean, not sex, just sleep. I thought we could see if we could sleep together. You know as if we were mates, sleep in the same bed kind of sleep."

"Yes, I understand," Alexander replied, smiling as he held out his hand. "I would like that very much."

I felt like a child, standing there and nodding repeatedly as I took his hand. He gently pulled me inside and closed the door behind me.

"I've never seen your room before."

"I don't believe I've ever seen yours either," Alexander replied with a nervous chuckle. That actually made me relax a bit. If he was nervous as well then at least

I wasn't the only one. "Um, how do you want to do this, Dimitri?"

"I don't know," I whispered looking into his eyes, knowing they must have been as wide as saucers I was so scared. "Maybe this was a mistake."

"No. Please don't go," he begged, tightening the grip he had on my hand. "Please, stay with me tonight."

"Okay."

"I really was just asking what side of the bed you wanted to sleep on," he said as he led me towards the bed. "I normally just sprawl out in the middle, so I don't have a preferred side."

"I normally sleep on the right side, because that's where my nightstand and alarm clock are. But I guess it really doesn't matter."

"No, no, you can have the right side," Alexander answered quickly as he pulled back the covers for me. "Please, go ahead and lay down."

"I-I don't normally . . ." I started to say and trailed off, swallowing loudly. My throat suddenly felt like I was in the middle of a desert.

"Don't normally what?"

"Sleep with clothes on," I answered so quickly the words ran into each other. It took him a second to register what I said, but when the look of surprise crossed his face I knew he'd heard me. "I'm sorry, I didn't mean to sound like a tease. I just realized that now, and I didn't know what to say or do when I did."

"No, of course you didn't," Alexander replied nodding. "I don't mean to start trouble, but I guess that means you never spent the night with Rune?"

I merely shook my head, not wanting to talk about Rune right at the moment. Instead we both climbed into bed. Most of the rooms in the main house came with full-sized beds. Sure, we could order bigger beds if we wanted to, I did since I'm so tall, but Alexander's was the standard size.

"Next time we should sleep in my bed," I chuckled breaking the ice. "I had an elongated queen size bed ordered so the mattress could fit me."

"That might be a good idea," he snickered. We both turned to look at each other then down at my calves and feet hanging off the bed, and we burst out laughing. When we finally stopped laughing Alexander started talking again. "There's something I want to say, but I don't want to ruin this moment."

"Go ahead, I'll try not to freak out."

"Are you sure?"

"No, but do it anyway. You should be able to say anything to your mate, and we're trying to really be mates."

"I love you, Dimitri," he said quietly, but kept talking before I could even reply. "I don't expect you to say it back, I understand why you won't. But it's the way I feel and I thought you should know. I really and truly love you. I think I have since I met you, even when you were a scrawny little pre-transition. There was just something about you, even at twenty-five."

"Why have you never told me before?" I wasn't so sure I really wanted to hear the answer, but I needed to know.

"At first, I wasn't even able to admit to myself I really felt that way about you," he answered looking off into the distance. "Then when it hit me that I was in love with you I knew it would be better for you if I hid it. I've been a warrior for so many centuries, killing and fighting Zakasacs. I resigned myself many, many centuries ago to the fact I wasn't ever going to fall in love. After all the death I've caused I don't deserve love."

"You talk as if you're a mass murderer, Alexander," I whispered as he turned to look at me. Searching his eyes I knew in my heart he believed what he said. "You killed to protect vampires, to help save the lives of our people. Not because you just randomly enjoyed killing people."

"How do you know I don't enjoy killing?"

"We all enjoy killing to a certain extent, or else we

wouldn't be warriors," I answered thoughtfully. "I mean, it's not the killing we like, but rather the fact the Zakasac died, not us. Not another vampire that the Zakasac would have killed."

"But killing is still killing, and I was raised to see killing as wrong," Alexander replied. "I always believed one hardened enough and cold enough to be a good warrior would never able to give love, or accept it."

"And now?"

"Now I want to love you, really love you and have you love me, more than I ever cared about being a warrior."

I didn't know what to say to his confession. The truth and pain was written all over his face. He was so ready for me to reject him at that moment. Instead I leaned in and kissed him. It was chaste at first, just a gentle press of our lips, but as we both leaned in again for another kiss it grew into something more.

"Wait, I said I wouldn't push you," he said breathlessly as he broke the kiss. "You came here for sleep, I didn't mean to start this."

"I'm okay with this," I answered honestly, running my fingers through his hair.

"You are?"

"Yes, if we can keep just kissing. I'm not ready for anything more than that, but it felt right to kiss you. I like having your arms around me, Alexander. I love knowing my scent is rubbing off on you, as if you're actually mine."

"I am yours, Dimitri," Alexander said before looking away from me. "I've not been with anyone since I've known that I was in love with you. It seemed wrong to be with another man when you had my heart."

"I didn't know," I whispered turning his face back towards mine. "I wish you had told me, I've loved you for probably just as long. It seems like so much wasted time."

"It wasn't wasted, even with all the mistakes I made. We still got to this point, here, together. We have all the time in the world ahead of us, we can make this work."

"I hope so." I moved to kiss him again. This time it was so passionate it was almost fierce. He shifted closer, and even with our height difference he felt so good against me. When Alexander moved his hand from my shoulder to my back, his hard cock pressed into my stomach. I moaned at the feeling of his hard-on against me, the knowledge he was this excited just from kissing me.

Without meaning to, or realizing I had, I was suddenly on top of him. My hips and lower body resting between his spread legs. I tore his shirt off him before pulling my own over my head. As we kept kissing, our tongues meshing and exploring, I reveled in the feeling of our naked chests rubbing against each other.

It was only when his hands moved from my back, one massaging my ass while the other moved towards the front of my shorts that I pulled away.

"I'm sorry, I can't," I said, starting to cry as I moved off of him and sat up. "I know I started this, but I can't. I want to believe you love me. I saw the truth of it on your face, but I also saw the truth when you said you didn't love me and didn't want me."

"You have nothing to be sorry for, Dimitri," he answered as he sat up and wrapped his arm around my shoulder. I let myself be pulled against him, "I did this. I put this distrust in you and you have every reason not to trust me. I don't know how, but somehow I will fix that."

"I'm sorry, I didn't mean to tease you. It just felt so good and so right, until . . ."

"Until I went too far," Alexander said gently.

"No, that's not what I was going to say," I replied shaking my head against him as he pulled us both down to the bed. "I gave you the green light to go there, it's just when I felt you touch me there, I thought of the last time you did . . . And that made me freeze up."

"The last time?" he asked sounding confused, but it must have clicked in his mind. "In the hallway, before I bit you."

"Yes." The tears started to fall. I felt like such an

idiot, crying against his chest. We were having such a good time and I had to go and blow it.

"I understand why that memory would have you pulling away from me," he said as if he had read my mind. "I am not upset with you, Dimitri. If you feel uncomfortable, you have every right to back away. And I want you to only feel good when I touch you."

"Thank you for understanding."

"Of course," he whispered, gently kissing my forehead. "Now we should sleep. It's been a very trying couple of weeks. I know you are still young, but I am a very old man who needs his rest."

"Whatever, you dork," I laughed before turning to press my lips against his chest. "Good night, Alexander."

"Good night, my Dimitri."

Even with all the pain he caused me over the weeks it still warmed my heart to hear him call me his Dimitri.

* * * *

I woke the next morning in the same position I had fallen asleep in the night before, with Alexander's steady heartbeat under my ear. At first it was a comforting sound, but then it started to sink in . . . what now? What did you say the morning after, especially when you didn't have sex?

"You awake?" I asked quietly.

"I have been for some time," he chuckled and I felt it rumble throughout his chest. It also struck me as odd that I slept on his chest when I was larger than he was. Didn't it normally go the smaller one curled up to the larger one? Or was it more an age thing? I really hoped the answer was it didn't matter and you just did what felt right.

"Um, what happens now?"

"We go about our day as normal, Dimitri."

"Oh, then why does this feel so weird?"

"This is your first time ever waking up in bed with another person, correct?" Alexander asked as he ran his head over my back.

"Yeah, it is," I replied and moved my head so I can look at his face. He was giving me one of those rare, full smiles.

"You don't know how much that pleases me, just because I'm a selfish man. It's normal that it would be awkward, given it's your first time," he answered. "There's no rule book here, Dimitri. Just like in sex and life, just do what feels right."

"Okay then," I said, smiling as I moved so I could kiss him. I planted a loud, goofy, smacking kiss on him and jumped out of bed. He looked at me with wide eyes before starting to laugh hysterically. I chuckled as well, while grabbing my shirt and pulling it on.

"Dimitri?"

"Yeah, Alex?" I replied, turning towards him. the look on his face when I called him Alex was priceless.

"Did you just call me, Alex?"

"I did, and I apologize. It just kind of came out."

"I actually like it coming from you," he answered smiling. "It warms my heart that you gave me a nickname."

"Okay, good. Then I'll call you Alex when it's just us."

"As you wish."

"Was there something you wanted to ask me?"

"Oh yes," he said quietly as he sat up in the bed. It was only then I realized I had been staring at his fabulous chest and stomach. I felt myself blush as I looked up and met his eyes. "I wanted to ask if we were going to be doing this again tonight?"

"I'd like that, I mean if you're okay with that."

"I'm more than just okay with it," he answered and gestured me to come towards him with his finger. I couldn't help smiling as I leaned over the bed and him. He pulled my head down and gave me another kiss. This one wasn't funny at all. This one melted me all the way to my toes.

"Wow," I said, like an idiot when we broke apart. "And on that note, I have to shower and get to class."

"Some morning, I would like to join you in the shower," he said gently. He said it in a way that let me know exactly what we would do in that shower, without trying to push me.

"I would like that one day," I replied as I opened the door. "And this time, I'm pushing you up against the wall and having my way with you." I hurried and left before he had a chance to reply. I knew it was kind of mean to push the boundaries like that, but damn, it was fun.

Racing back to my room, I showered and changed in under five minutes. I was at the gym for class in less than ten. Once there, the instructors helped me match up students of like abilities for sparring practice.

"What's with you today?" Matteo leaned in and asked as we watched the student work.

"Alexander and I slept together last night," I answered quietly. I almost laughed at the shocked expression on his face, "we didn't have sex. We slept, literally."

"Are you okay?"

"Yeah, actually, I am. It was time to take the next step."

"Good, I'm glad," Matteo replied cautiously, searching my face. "If he hurts you again, I'm still going to cut off his dick in his sleep and give it to you."

It was then I heard a chuckle from across the gym. We both looked over to see Alexander leaning one shoulder against the wall, smiling and watching us. Matteo turned bright red and I had to bite my lip so as not to laugh.

Later, at breakfast, I saw Alexander watching me again, just smiling. I couldn't help but smile back. It was good, this feeling I had inside. It was almost like a warmth building around my heart. So is this what it felt like to be loved?

Chapter 9

After lunch I was heading back to my office, looking over papers, when I bumped into Rune. Oh shit, this was so not a conversation I wanted to have right now.

"Hey, Rune," I said, starting to fidget.

"Dimitri," he replied, nodding at me then started to continue on his way. I let out the breath I was holding, it looked like I averted that particular land mine. Until he turned back around, "so it was never me you wanted to be with, was it?"

"It's not that I didn't want to be with you. I was trying to move on."

"From Alexander?"

"Yeah, from him."

"But now you're mated to him, right?" He asked me, raising an eyebrow. "Unless I've heard the latest rumors wrong."

"He mated me, I've not mated him yet," I answered scrunching my eyebrows down. "I'm not sure if that makes a difference in your mind, but I just don't want to lie to you."

"Again you mean. You don't want to lie to me again?"

"When did I lie to you the first time?" I asked as I started to get pissy. "I never made you any promises, Rune. You were in it for the uncomplicated fuck, just as I was."

"I was?" he replied, seeming to get just as upset. "I didn't know it was just an uncomplicated fuck."

"We never even kissed, Rune. It was just fucking, kinky and casual fucking."

"Maybe to you. I thought I finally found a dom who wanted my type of submissive," he answered not meeting my eyes. "But you were just using me because I look like him from the back."

"One, we were using each other. Two, yeah, it helped me that you look like Alexander from the back. But you came to me, Rune. I didn't come seek you out."

"So what?" He yelled looking me in the eyes. "Just because I sought you out, it's okay to treat me that way?"

"What way? We didn't date, hell we barely talked. All we did was fuck a few times," I snarled. Then it hit me I had really hurt him, and that was never my intention. "Look, Rune, it wasn't ever my intention to use you. Alexander said he didn't want me. And in my mind, I thought if I could start having sex with someone, it would help me move on."

"But it didn't, did it?"

"No, it didn't. I came to you when I got your note, and I couldn't even get hard," I answered shaking my head as I ran my fingers through my hair. "And it wasn't because of you, I mean, you're a good looking guy, Rune. It was more a mental or emotional thing for me. You weren't Alexander."

"But you did get hard, I mean you fucked me," he said, looking totally confused.

"When I realized you looked like him," I replied sheepishly looking at my feet. "If I had known it was more than just uncomplicated sex to you I would never have done what we did. But truly, I thought we were just both scratching an itch. The sex I had with Alexander after I lost the challenge was my first time. So, I know it's not an excuse, but it's the reason I seemed to have missed that you thought maybe we had more."

"Well that makes sense," Rune answered nodding. "I thought you were just thinking I wasn't worth keeping. Or you didn't respect me enough to care about my feelings."

"Rune, no!" I replied completely shocked at his words, "I'd never just disregard someone's feelings like that! I really thought you didn't want any more than just the sex. If I'd had any idea you wanted more, I would never,

ever have treated you like that. I'm sorry, Rune."

"You don't have to be sorry, Dimitri. Like you said, you didn't know any better. You're not part of the dominant/submissive game. And now you're mated to Alexander, so you can have your happily ever after."

"I hope so, but I'm not so sure," I answered feeling stupid talking about feeling with Rune. It wasn't the type of conversation we had ever had. "I want to believe that this is forever, but I keep waiting for the other shoe to drop. Does that make sense?"

"Yeah, it makes perfect sense," Rune answered as he patted me on the back. "You're a good guy, I do truly hope it works out for you."

"You too, Rune. Anyone would be lucky to be with you."

"I'm not so sure about that, you know the type of sex I'm into," Rune said, looking distraught. "Most people would or have called me a freak and left. You were one of the first who seemed to be into it."

"I think I'm too new to sex to really know what I'm into."

"Yeah, I remember those days," he laughed as he started to walk away again. "See you around, Dimitri."

"Later, Rune," I answered, looking back at my papers and shaking my head. Well at least that hadn't gone as bad as I thought it was going to.

"So you really slept with him because you could pretend it was me?" Alexander asked as he stepped out of the other hallway into view. I closed my eyes and took a deep breath before simply nodding. I mean, what else could I do? How did I explain this one to Alexander?

I kept waiting to hear his footsteps retreat, instead I got shoved into the wall. Surprised I opened my eyes in time to see Alexander lean in to kiss me. I melted against the wall and his firm body as he made love to my mouth.

"I thought you never really loved me if you could have moved on so easily," he said when we parted. I watched tears fall down his cheeks, too shocked at seeing him cry to answer. "But you never really moved on, did you? You tried because I told you I didn't want you, but you couldn't move on?"

"No, I couldn't," I whispered, "I love you too much."

"As I love you," he answered

Both of us were crying now. Alexander leaned closer to kiss me again, working his way down my chin, then towards my neck. Just as I felt him lick the spot where he normally bit me, I pulled away.

"I can't," I cried. "I'm sorry, but I just can't do this."

"But you love me," Alexander replied, looking

confused and hurt. "And I love you."

"I know, but I'm just not ready for this yet. And especially not in his hallway!"

I saw it click in his head which hallway we were standing in and his whole attitude change. "I understand, Dimika. Please just hear me when I say that I love you, because I do, with my whole heart."

"Okay," I replied as I untangled my body from his. "I need to go."

"We're still on for tonight, right?"

"Yeah, tonight is fine. I'll see you at my room sometime after dinner."

"Looking forward to it, Dimitri," Alexander said, smiling. "And just sleep, I know."

I was only able to give him half a smile as I nodded and turned to head to my office.

* * * *

Sitting in my office the next day I thought back to the night before. It was the second night in a row Alexander and I shared a bed. Nothing much past first base happened, but it was comfortable and it felt right for us to sleep in the same bed. The thought made me smile that goofy smile you get in the beginning of a relationship when everything is going well.

"Hey, Dimitri, we have a problem," Yuri said as he walked through the door. "Alexander was working with Lance and ended up in the clinic with wounds from a sword."

"What?" I yelled and in one motion was up and over the desk. Pushing past Yuri, I flew through the gym and outside.

No, this wasn't happening! We just got somewhere and now this was happening. What scared me the most was that I couldn't feel him. We were mates! Shouldn't that entail me to some privileges, like knowing if he was alive?

I don't think I ever ran as fast as I did that day to the clinic. It wasn't until I hit the clinic's doors that I realized I had tears streaming down my face. God, I loved him so fucking much, I couldn't lose him. I wouldn't survive it. I should have told him I loved him, not just admitted it after he heard me talking with Rune.

Skidding to a halt, I heard Alexander's voice inside one of the rooms in the clinic.

"I said I'm fine," Alexander grumbled, pushing one of the clinic attendants away from him. "It's just a few scratches."

He looked at me as I stepped into the room. The expression on his face let me know exactly what I looked like right then.

"Come here, Dimika," he said gently as he held his arms open to me. I took the last few steps quickly and carefully let him hold me. "I'm fine, I swear. Lance just stepped out of line with the swords."

"That little bastard, I'm going to gut him like a fish," I growled as my hands roamed his body. I needed to see and feel for myself that he was okay. "You really are okay then?"

"I'm fine and Lance has a hearing with the council for his little revenge attempt," Alexander chuckled. "I sent Yuri to tell you, I figured you should know, you being in charge of training and all."

"God, when he told me you were hurt," I started to say, choking up. I sat on the edge of his bed and looked at the other people in the room. With one of his looks at the doctor the man hurried everyone out of the room. I turned back to Alexander, "I was so scared I'd never get the chance to tell you that I love you."

"You told me last night," Alexander replied taking my face in his hands. "I love you too, Dimika."

"No, I admitted it last night after you heard me talking with Rune. That's different than just telling you," I said, the tears starting again. "I love you, Alexander. I've never loved anyone else, and I never want anyone else. I want you as my mate in every way possible. I'm yours, just don't ever leave me or scare me like that again."

"I won't, baby, I swear."

"I'm sorry I've been such a pain," I stated leaning more into his embrace.

"Why are you sorry, baby? I put us here, you have nothing to be sorry for."

"Is this the only wound?" I asked gently touching the small gash on his shoulder that was already mostly healed.

"Yes, it was one swipe of the sword and the kid was lucky even to get that," Alexander explained. Then he grabbed me roughly and pulled my mouth down to his. The kiss was desperate, filled with everything unsaid, not to mention every emotion flowing through the both of us.

Without breaking the kiss, I ripped the medical gown off of him. I stopped kissing him then to take in the glorious, naked body before me. "No one else will ever see you like this, or touch you, or I will snap off your balls and feed them to you."

"No one, Dimika. I want only you," he whispered before kissing me again. "And I want something from you that I've never asked anyone before."

"What is it?" I asked as I stood and pulled off my shorts. "You're alive and mine, you could ask me for my dick and I'd give it to you right now."

"Actually I was going to ask for you to put it in my ass."

"Huh?" I said, looking up completely confused. I'm sure I looked a sight, standing there with my shorts around my ankles, about to pull my shirt off my head.

"I've never let anyone take my ass before," Alexander explained as he moved off the bed. "I want you to be my first and only. I want to feel that huge cock in my ass and then your bite as you make me yours for eternity."

"Really?" I squeaked out looking down into the eyes of the man I loved. "Are you sure?"

"More sure than I've ever been in my entire life," he replied as he grabbed my hardening cock and started stroking it. I moaned and claimed his lips. Then in one swift motion, I spun him around and bent him over the bed. I knelt down behind him and spread the cheeks of his ass. Leaning forward I used my tongue to rim his tight hole."

"Oh fuck, Dimika," Alexander screamed, his body squirming under the assault of my tongue. I grabbed some lotion from the nightstand by the hospital bed. As I kept licking and eating his ass I squirted some of it on my fingers. Just to keep Alexander guessing, I slid my middle finger in his ass as I pulled out my tongue.

I moved to stand behind him while I wiggled my

finger in his ass, stretching him out so that he was ready for my cock. "This ass is mine. Do I make myself perfectly clear, Alexander?"

"Yes, Dimika, I am yours. Always yours, forever," he cried out as I slipped another finger in him. "Oh god, I never knew it could be like this. It's too much."

"Just ride it, Alex," I cooed in his ear as I scissored my fingers. "I've got you, baby. I won't let you fall."

"I love you, Dimika," he moaned as I pushed in a third finger. "Fuck me, my Dimika. I want that beautiful cock in my ass."

"Ask and you shall receive," I snickered as I pulled my fingers free and squirted some lotion on my dick. I groaned as Alexander reached back and pulled the cheeks of his ass apart for me. I didn't waste any time moving in behind him. Guiding my cock into his hole, he moaned in pleasure as I pushed past the first ring. I bit my lip as I paused to allow him to adjust to my size.

"Why did you stop?" he asked as he looked over his shoulder, confusion all over his face.

"I'm just pausing so I don't hurt you," I answered as I kissed up his back.

"It doesn't hurt, it feels fantastic. You won't hurt me, Dimika. Take me, make me your mate."

"I so love you," I groaned as I took him at his word

and pushed all the way in. We both moaned as I bottomed out in his ass. I reached up and grabbed his shoulders for leverage and started a hard and fast pace.

"So... fucking... good... love... your... cock... in... my... ass," Alexander grunted out in between my thrusts. His words and the sounds from him spurred me on. It never felt like this with Rune. It was like our souls were aligning. Everything in me sang for me to lean over and bite him.

"Are you sure this is what you want?" I leaned over his back and whispered in his ear, fucking him hard all the while.

"Yes, claim me."

He screamed as I licked the side of his neck. I struck as I felt the muscles in his ass start to spasm. He roared so loudly the windows shook and the muscles in his ass clamped down on my cock. I knew he climaxed just as his blood hit my tongue. Tasting my mate for the first time pushed me right over the edge with him.

I can't even explain the wonderful taste of my mate's live essence in my mouth. It was like the best aged wine with chocolate covered strawberries all wrapped in one. Combine that with the sensations of my cock being wrapped in Alexander's ass. His muscles milked every last drop of cum out of me.

"Promise you will never leave me or fuck with my

head again," I whispered as I collapsed on top of him.

"Never again, Dimika," he answered panting. "My love will always be honest from now on. Never again will my love be full of deceit."

I knew at that moment he was telling me the truth. I had finally found my happily ever after and it just so happened to be in the arms of my legendary, Russian warrior.

THE END

LOVE'S

INDECISION

WARRIOR CAMP, BOOK 2

JOYEE FLYNN

SILVER PUBLISHING
Published by Silver Publishing
Publisher of Erotic Romance

To my Yahoo Group:

You guys fucking rock!

Thanks for pushing me so hard to get this book done.

Your love and support make being an author fun.

CHAPTER 1

"Mind if I join you?" A voice asked, pulling me out of the calm, relaxing shower I was taking. Opening my eyes I saw Nate Hathus standing a few feet in front of me. He was completely naked, gorgeous, and my student.

"Why are you in the instructor's shower room, Nate?" I asked, turning from where I was leaning my back against the cool tile to facing it instead. I couldn't talk to him when we were both naked like this, plus I needed to hide my now raging hard-on.

"Our showers were full," Nate purred, turning on the shower next to me. I froze when his hip brushed against my ass. "Besides, it seemed a shame to know you were in here wet and naked and not get to watch."

"Don't do this, Nate," I answered, angling my body so my back was to him once again. "I think you should go."

"You don't want me to leave, do you Matteo?"

No, I really didn't. But Nate was twenty-four, and while he'd be considered an adult in the human world, in our world it meant he hadn't even gone through his transition yet. We didn't transition into full vampires and come into our powers until midnight of our twenty-fifth birthday. And while I wanted Nate more than I needed my next breath, he was my student and as such, off limits.

"Yes, please go," I whispered as I felt him move closer, the heat from his body causing me to shake. Instead of listening, Nate placed his hand on my side and started massaging my hip. I wasn't able to keep the groan from passing my lips.

"You want me as much as I want you, Matteo," Nate answered, stepping so close I felt his hard cock press against my thigh.

"Why do you deny it?"

"Because you're my student," I replied, stepping away from him. "You're too young to know what you want, Nate."

"I'm not some wide-eyed virgin," Nate snapped. Just the idea of someone else touching him, being with him, set me off. In a flash I had him against the wall, my entire body pressed flush against his. My hands were on either side of his head as I leaned in so close our noses touched.

"Who have you been with, Nate?" I growled possessively. I knew it was wrong, and that I shouldn't care. He wasn't mine to have. But the beautiful man in front of me was my Achilles' heel, had been from the moment I first met him. "Who has touched you? I will fucking kill them."

"No one you know," Nate panted as his hands moved to my hips and pulled me closer.

The instant our cocks brushed together I was done for. I mashed my mouth down on his, finally tasting the sweet lips I'd been dreaming of. Nate parted his lips as he moaned, so I slid my tongue into his mouth to explore him. He tasted even better than I could have ever imagined.

He yelped when I pulled his legs up and wrapped them around my hips. Taking advantage of it, I claimed his mouth again. Demanding his submission, I took everything he had to offer me. "You shouldn't play with fire, Nate."

"I want to be burned by you," he moaned as he started to kiss the side of my neck. "Please don't deny us this anymore, Matteo."

"Fuck," I groaned as he began biting on my earlobe. I shook as his hands roamed my back, loving the feel of the smaller man finally in my arms. "Be sure this is what you want, Nate. My control is not limitless."

"Fuck me, Matteo," Nate hissed in my ear, making my cock twitch against his. "I want you pounding my ass. I need to feel your cock inside me."

Any rational thought left in my head flew out the window. Reaching over to one of the shelves, I grabbed the shampoo. It wasn't lube but it would work for now. I squeezed some on my hands before dropping it back on the shelf and moving them to his ass. Slowly, I slid a finger into his tight hole as he cried out and shook in my arms. Bracing us against the shower wall gave me the leverage I needed to hold Nate while still being able to stretch him out.

"I've wanted this for so long," I whispered against his lips before delving back into that sweet mouth. He moaned and wrapped his legs tighter around me as I slipped a second finger into his hole. I almost regretted not being able to take the time to lick and rim his ass with my tongue, but there was no way I would have the control for that much foreplay.

"Please hurry, Matteo," Nate whimpered as he licked the side of my neck. "I need to have you in me."

"Okay, baby," I answered, quickly pushing in a third finger and moving them around to stretch him out. I had the same need to be in him as he had for me to take him.

"I'm not going to last much longer," he panted, pulling his head back to look into my eyes. The fierceness of need I could see there was amazing. "Fuck me now. Please, Matteo, I'm ready."

Instead, I rubbed the tips of my fingers over his sweet spot as I kept stretching him out. I watched, completely enthralled, as he stiffened in my arms before his cock exploded against my stomach. Nate cried out loudly, moving his hips so that he impaled himself further on my fingers and rubbed his dick against my abs.

"We should stop here," I said as I leaned forward and touched our foreheads together when he came down from his climax. "This shouldn't have happened."

"You wanted it to as much as I did," Nate said, still trying to catch his breath. "I don't want to stop. I want you to fuck me like you've never fucked anyone before."

"Nate, don't push me," I growled, desperately wanting to do what he said. Instead I pulled my fingers out of him and let him slide down until his feet touched the floor. "This is wrong. We can't do this."

"It's not wrong," Nate yelled, shocking me down to my core. I'd never heard him raise his voice before, especially not to me. "Fine, I'm all stretched and ready to go. If you won't fuck me, I'm sure I can find someone else who will."

He didn't get more than two steps away from me before I was on him again. The idea of someone else touching him, especially after what we just shared, had me seeing red.

"You want me to fuck you, Nate?"

"Yes, I want you, Matteo," he panted, unable to move, seeing as I had his chest pinned against the wall. My body surrounded his smaller one completely as I held us both facing the tile. "And you want me."

"God help me, I do," I answered as I lined up my cock with his perfect little hole. Gently, I pushed in, stopping after passing the first ring. "You're so fucking tight, Nate."

"I said I wasn't a virgin," Nate seemed to have trouble talking, "I didn't say I'd had anyone in my ass before."

"I'm your first?" I asked, a thrill shooting through my entire body at the idea of being the only person in the man before me. "I should have prepared you more."

"It feels perfect, Matteo," he replied, turning to smile at me over his shoulder. "You're a perfect fit."

"Fuck," I groaned, loving that little smile of his and the fact that I was pleasing him. Not being able to hold still any longer I pushed more of my cock into him. I slowly worked it in and out of his very tight ass, grabbing his hips once I had worked more than halfway into him. "So fucking tight. Your ass is like heaven."

Nate moaned, turning his head to the side so that his cheek was against the tile. He reached back and grabbed my hips, pulling me to him. "Harder, Matteo. Don't hold back, take me."

"As you wish," I purred, licking his lips before pulling back and slamming my cock all the way into him. We both moaned loudly when I was seated all the way in. When I started moving again my pace was fast and hard. Nate moved his hands to brace himself against the wall as I grunted and pounded my cock into him.

"Fuck, you're so huge," Nate cried out. "Slam that massive cock into me."

I just about swallowed my tongue as his dirty words caused my cock to twitch inside of him. I didn't think I could fuck him any harder, but I was wrong. The force of my thrusts was too much for a virgin ass but I had no reason or control left.

Just as I was getting close I licked the side of his neck, wanting to sink my fangs into his tender skin. He smelled so fucking good.

"Bite me, Matteo," Nate moaned. "Make me yours forever."

That got my attention. I hadn't realized until he said it, but that was exactly what I wanted. Turning my head away from his neck I reached around in front of him and grabbed his hard dick. It only took a few strokes with my hand before he screamed, coming all over my hand and the shower wall. The muscles in his perfect ass clamped down on my cock.

"Fuck!" I roared as I climaxed, shooting my load into Nate. I kept thrusting my hips into him hard, drawing out my orgasm. When my dick was finally spent we slumped to the ground until I was sitting on my heels, Nate's back pressed against my chest, his tight ass still around my cock. After a few moments of post orgasmic bliss the guilt started to set in.

I pulled Nate off my lap and moved to sit with my back against the wall. Resting my head against my knees, I tried desperately to catch my breath.

"What's wrong, Matteo?" Nate asked kneeling in front of me.

"Oh nothing," I snorted. "I just fucked one of my students and almost claimed him. I am fan-fucking-tastic."

"There's nothing wrong with what we did," Nate whispered, almost as if trying to convince himself more than me.

"It can never happen again," I answered, making sure I was looking him right in the eye. "I mean that, Nate. Don't ever come to me like this again."

"You don't mean that," Nate gasped, dropping the hand he'd stretched out to me. "Matteo, don't do this."

"I'm stopping this before it starts," I replied, shaking my head. "This was a mistake, a horrible mistake."

"I'm not a mistake," Nate whispered as he started to back away from me. "Don't do this, Matteo. Don't take this away from us."

"There is no *us*, Nate," I said firmly, knowing in my heart it was a lie. There was very much an 'us', and I wanted there to be. "This should never have happened."

"You don't mean that."

"I do mean that, Nate," I replied, squaring my shoulders to leave no room for argument. "This was a mistake, it will never happen again. I won't ever touch you again, Nate."

"No," Nate whispered. Tears started to fall down his cheeks. Seeing the pain I was causing him made me want to do nothing but pull him into my arms and comfort him. But I knew this was best for him. Nate had so much promise, and was so young. He didn't need to be tied to a centuries-old warrior, he needed to explore life. I couldn't let him miss out on that, no matter how much I wanted him.

"I'm sorry I let this happen," I said as I got to my feet. I reached out a hand to help Nate up. He looked at it like it was a snake before his gaze went back to my eyes.

"It wasn't a mistake," he sniffled as he got to his feet without my help and backed away. "I'm not sorry it happened, so don't you dare apologize."

Before I could say anything else, he turned and ran from the showers. I stood there like an idiot, unable to move. It felt as if my heart had been ripped out of my chest and gone with him. Turning, I went to clean up in the water. I sighed as I washed Nate's cum off my hand and his scent off my body. It felt more like I was washing away the best thing that ever happened to me.

Shutting off the water, I grabbed a towel and dried off. Never mind that being with Nate was the best sex I could ever remember having. Even if I ignored how much I wanted to claim him, make him mine forever, it hurt to wash him off me. I would have loved to walk around smelling like the gorgeous, wonderful man I just hurt.

CHAPTER 2

The next few days I went through the motions of my responsibilities knowing my heart wasn't into it. Nate avoided me like the plague, not that I blamed him. Even my best friend was starting to notice. The third day, I looked up from my work to see Dimitri standing in the doorway of my office looking extremely pissed off.

"Want to explain why my best instructor and student are walking around like zombies?" he growled as he came into the office and shut the door. "Start talking, Matteo. I gave you guys a few days, hoping this would resolve itself. But no more. I'm officially sticking my nose into this."

"I fucked up," I answered quietly, dropping my head in my hands. "I so fucked up, Dimitri."

"You slept with him, didn't you?"

The lump that formed in my throat was so large I couldn't talk. Instead I just looked at him and nodded, feeling the tears burning in my eyes.

"Fuck, Matteo!" Dimitri yelled. "How can I be pissed with you when you're obviously hurting? Tell me what happened?"

"The little siren cornered me in the shower," I choked out, wiping my eyes. "I lost all control and fucked him against the shower wall."

"It was… I mean… Nate agreed to it, right?"

It took me a minute to get what Dimitri was hinting at. When I did, I saw red. "I would never rape him! Of course it was fucking consensual."

"Okay. Okay, Matteo," he said quietly, holding his hands out in front of him in surrender. "I'm just trying to figure out why this is such a big deal? So, you guys finally had sex. I've been waiting for that to happen for months, I know you love him."

His statement hit me like a ton of bricks. I knew I lusted after Nate, but love? Did I love Nate?

"I can see the look on your face, dude," Dimitri said as he took a seat in front of my desk. "Yes, you love Nate. It's written all over you every time you look at him."

"God, I'm a selfish bastard," I replied, letting my head thump on the desk. "I do love him. Which makes me believe even more that I'm doing the right thing; I should never have touched him, though."

"Okay, so you guys had sex in the shower, then what?"

"I told him it was a mistake and that it would never happen again."

"You're a fucking idiot, you know that, right?" Dimitri grumbled. "You're pulling the same shit Alexander pulled on me. And you saw how well that went."

"It's not the same," I replied, defending myself. "He's just a kid. My student, for god's sake. Nate's not even hit his transition; he can't know what he wants."

"He's not a kid, Matteo," Dimitri said, running his fingers through his hair and taking a deep breath. "Yes, he's not transitioned yet, but he's not a child. Nate loves you, and you love him. I'm not really seeing why this is confusing for you."

"He deserves better than some centuries-old warrior. Nate's young, and full of life," I answered shaking my head. "You know how we change after our transitions, he might not even be the same man."

"That's bullshit, and you know it," Dimitri replied, smacking his hand on the top of the desk and looking like he wished it were me. "Yeah, we change after our transitions, but not our core personality.

And no one said anything about mating for eternity with Nate, just be with him."

"Yeah, no one mentioned mating," I laughed. At first it was just a chuckle, but it turned into a hysterical, 'I've lost my mind' kind of laugh. Then the laughs turned into sobs and I thunked my head back down on the desk… repeatedly.

"Talk to me, Matteo," Dimitri said gently as he rubbed my back. I hadn't even heard him move from where he was seated. "I can't help you if you won't talk to me."

"Like you talked to me when you were having problems with Alexander?"

"One, it was Alexander jerking me around," he answered, going very still. "Two, you're right, I should have talked to you about it. I realized that after things got better. Maybe if I'd had the help of my best friend before everything got so out of control, things would have turned out differently."

That got me to lift my head and look at him. I could see the stark honesty on Dimitri's face. "You never told me that."

"I was embarrassed," he replied, shrugging. "I was humiliated when it was happening, and embarrassed afterwards that I didn't have the balls to seek help. You have no idea how many times since Alexander and I worked things out that I wished I'd sought you out earlier."

"Thanks, that means a lot to me," I answered. In a surprising move, I stood and hugged my best friend. At first he was stiff in my arms but then he hugged me back. "I thought I failed you as a friend. All I kept thinking about was what I had done wrong to cause you not to trust me, why you wouldn't confide in me."

"It wasn't you, Matteo. You're like a brother to me, always

have been," Dimitri said, rubbing my back as we kept hugging. "Don't make the same mistakes I did, brother. Talk to me."

"It wasn't just the sex," I whispered, clutching onto my friend as if he was the only thing real in my world. "I didn't realize I was doing it, but I was licking his neck as if to prepare to mate him. Nate told me to bite him, make him mine forever, and that snapped me out of it."

Dimitri didn't say anything, just kept rubbing my back as if waiting for me to continue.

"Once you've had the urge to bite your mate, it won't go away," Alexander said from the doorway. "Believe me, I know."

"How long have you been there?" I asked, looking up from Dimitri's shoulder.

"Long enough to know you're struggling with the same thing I did," he answered, looking at his feet. "I'm sorry I was eavesdropping, but I was looking for my mate. When I saw him in your arms I almost came in and ripped off your head."

"I was just comforting my friend," Dimitri said, not letting me go.

"I realized that and calmed down," Alexander replied nodding. "But when I heard what you were talking about, it was like hearing my own thoughts from a few months ago. I didn't even mean to stand here and listen, but it was like I couldn't leave."

"I'm not upset, Alexander," I answered moving out of Dimitri's arms. "You're right. If anyone understands where I'm at, it's you."

"Thank you," he replied, sitting in of the chairs. I watched him rub his chin, as if thinking on how to proceed. "I agree our circumstances are different, Nate being pre-trans and all. But, you need to have enough faith in the man you love to talk to him, Matteo. Nate is a good man, he deserves to know how you're feeling."

"You mean, tell him I think I'm just some washed-up warrior not worthy of him?" I asked chuckling. "Oh yeah, I can see that conversation going well."

"Hey, that's my best friend you're talking about," Dimitri said, smacking me upside the head. "I think Alexander means telling Nate about your fears of him changing his mind after his transition."

"As always, you are very astute, my love," Alexander replied as he smiled at his mate. How I longed to have someone look at me like Alexander was staring at Dimitri, as if his whole life was wrapped up in my best friend. "Your concerns are valid; while Nate is a man and not a child, he will be different after his transition. That doesn't mean it can't work out between the two of you, it's just something you have to address."

"Neither of you think it's wrong for me to have been with a student?" I asked, looking between the both of them. "How can you not hate me? I hate myself for what I did."

"It's one thing if you were just fucking your way through the class," Dimitri answered, looking at me with so much sympathy it almost hurt. "But you love Nate."

"Which is why it can't ever happen again," I replied.

"But you need to tell him why," Alexander said, reaching for Dimitri. They clasped hands and turned back to me. "Trying to get Nate to hate you isn't the way to handle this. I almost destroyed Dimitri, and myself, by making that mistake. We were lucky I finally pulled my head out of my ass, mainly because of your help, Matteo. Don't make the same mistake I did."

"Thank you," I answered, nodding. "I'll think about what you said, I promise."

"Good, because I'm really concerned about Nate's state of mind," Dimitri said as he pulled Alexander to his feet. "I can attest to the fact that the grief Nate is going through will swarm him like nothing else."

"I told him us being together was a mistake. I hurt him, just as Alexander said, thinking that if he hated me it would be easier for him," I stated, looking at my feet.

"God, Matteo," Dimitri sighed. "I know you're hurting, and that you thought what you were doing was the best thing for him. But I've been on the receiving end of that sort of thing and I can tell you, it made me feel as if life wasn't worth living."

"I'll fix this, I promise," I replied, remembering how badly Alexander pushing Dimitri away had hurt him. It was stupid of me to ever think it was the right way to handle Nate. Both men looked me over before nodding, and then they turned and left my office.

I sat down in the chair behind my desk, ready to do some serious thinking, but just then, my phone rang. I answered it. "Yeah?"

"Matteo, it's Rune," the man said into the other end of the line. "Lance just started his transition. Tonight's his birthday."

"Alright, I'm on my way," I replied, hanging up the phone. As much as I hated the little shit, the transition was horrible and painful. I stood up, grabbing my bag before locking up my office and heading towards the infirmary.

The camp had housing for the warriors, which was like a mansion where we all lived in our own private suites. There were also the student dorms, which were like dorm rooms at a college. Then it had several gyms, the mess hall, infirmary, the arena, and quite a few obstacle courses for training.

The warrior camp isn't like ancient warrior camps

were, though there are still some of the old traditions. It's more like a human military base, but it comes complete with battles for dominance as of old. A warrior can challenge another for several reasons. One being to show they are now stronger and willing to fight for a higher rank amongst us. Or it could just be an everyday argument that results in a challenge.

Whatever the reason is for one to occur, challenge fights are not like normal sparring, ever. It's all about dominance and who is stronger, better. You can either take the challenge, or yield. If someone yields they acknowledge their opponent as superior, and higher in ranking, than themselves. If a challenge is accepted the combatants fight until someone is defeated. The loser not only gives their rank to the winner, but their body as well.

To put it bluntly, the winner has the right to fuck the loser. It's a part of the older traditions, showing the winner is not only the strongest and best, but also demeaning the loser in public, stripping them of their rank and dignity. It's hard to hold onto any shred of pride when you lose a fight and immediately get fucked on your hands and knees in front of all the spectators.

Reaching the dorms, I snapped back into the present and jogged up to the infirmary. With the workouts the pre-trans, post-trans, and warriors went through daily a state-of-the-art medical facility was a must have. When I got to the main room of the infirmary, which was also used as a trauma room, I could see Lance strapped down to a bed. The poor guy was already screaming so loudly it hurt my ears.

If there was ever a student I wanted to take outside and hang from the nearest tree by his nuts, it was Lance. Born of a wealthy, older warrior family, he had a chip on his shoulder that he seemed to have had since birth. Unfortunately, his attitude made me want to take that chip and brain him with it. But, no matter my feelings towards Lance, going through your transition is one of the most horrible moments of a vampire's life.

On top of which, it was worse for vampires destined to be warriors. It's not all that hard to determine at birth if a vampire will grow to be a warrior or not. First, we're born early; usually popping out of our mothers after seven months, not the normal nine. Also, warriors are unusually large babies when they're born.

Most vampires look like scrawny, underfed children until their transitions. Pre-trans warriors, however, look more like humans and post-transition vampires. When the transition hits, vampires and warriors alike grow at accelerated rates for eight or so hours, causing horrifying amounts of pain.

As Lance continued to scream in pain and the

medical staff gave him a shot of painkillers and sedatives, I thought back to my own transition several centuries ago. It was before there was any medicine available to help alleviate the pain. The worst part was, some vampires didn't make it. I had been so close to becoming one of the few who didn't make it.

The middle of three children, I'd always been invisible to my family unless I was in trouble. My parents hadn't even explained to me what the transition was or what I would go through. Since I was already the same size as some of my family and friends, I had no idea what was going to happen to me the day before my twenty-fifth birthday. When the cramps started all over my body I was scared I was dying.

I remember moving as fast I could, through the pain, to find my mother. When I told her what was happening she rolled her eyes and told me I was transitioning. She yelled at me for interrupting her day and said to go to my room, I would either live through it or not. That was the first time I realized how little my parents really cared about me.

"Matteo, he's calm for now," one of the doctors told me as he walked past me and out of the room. I nodded and headed over to Lance's bed. As much I as I hated the little shit, my heart went out to him knowing the hours of pain still before him.

"Am I going to die?" Lance asked before groaning in pain and curling into a ball.

"No, this is normal, Lance," I answered, reaching over to rub the boy's back. "It will pass, just breathe through the pain."

"Fuck," he gasped as another wave of pain shot through him. I watched in astonishment as his body grew at least an inch. No matter how many transitions I witness, it always amazes me how fast the process happens. "Please, just kill me, Matteo."

"Can't do it, Lance," I whispered thinking back to how many warriors over the years had asked me that same thing. "Just keep breathing."

"What comes next?" Lance asked with tears in his eyes.

"You've been taught what to expect."

"I can't think through the pain. Please, Matteo, I'm begging you, walk me through it," he sobbed. Again I took pity on the man, knowing most of the reason Lance was such an asshole was his upbringing. I'd met his parents briefly, once; they made Lance look like a saint.

"First, your bones will grow," I said, pulling up a

chair to sit next to him. Once I was comfortable in the seat, I continued. "Then your muscles and skin will grow as well to accommodate your new, larger size. After which, every vessel and organ will do the same. The last stage doesn't hurt like the rest, but the fever that will take you will feel like you're sitting on the sun."

"Right, first the cramping, then the pain from the bones growing," he replied as everything he'd be taught resurfaced. "The muscles and skin are more a cramping and pulling dull pain. Then the fevers, after which is the skull-smashing pain of my fangs growing in."

"You'll make it through this, Lance," I cooed, trying to keep him calm. "Just remember to keep breathing, slow, deep breaths. All you can do is breathe and remember not to panic. If things start going south, I promise you that I will tell you. Your parents have been called, though I'm sure they knew this was coming."

"They said they'll stop by tomorrow once they have word I made it," Lance said, tears running down his face. "Is that how all parents react?"

"No, it's not," I answered honestly. "You have people here though, and that's more than I had for my transition."

"Will you tell me about it?"

I looked at Lance's face for a few moments. When I realized the pre-trans really was looking for a distraction, and not just being an ass, I told him about how my mother reacted when I told her what was happening. Then I told him how my family hadn't even warned me about the transition.

"God, and I thought my parents were assholes," he whispered. "But you made it, of course."

"I did," I answered nodding. "They didn't have painkillers or shots back then, but I made it. I went to my little corner of the room I shared with my siblings. The only time I remember seeing my family during it was when my father came into the room and screamed at me for making so much noise. He said if the transition didn't kill me, he would if I didn't shut my trap."

"Do you still talk to your parents?"

"No, not since after my transition," I explained. "When it was finally over, a warrior they had sent for came into the room. He freaked out when he saw that no one was attending to me and no one had given me any blood. His name was Renaldo. He picked me up in his arms and carried me outside to his carriage. Next thing I knew we were driving to somewhere, not that I knew or cared where. Along the way we stopped and picked up a human and he helped me drink from them."

"Wow, before they had blood banks," he said with his eyes wide. "I forgot you're that old."

"Yeah, no bags of blood back then," I chuckled. "Back then you learned how to hunt and wipe human minds of the memories of you drinking from them, or you starved. Thankfully, Renaldo handled it that time and then worked with me, teaching me how to do it. He said I was lucky to have made it though my transition, given my parents hadn't even supplied me with blood after my fangs grew in."

"Guess I sound like a whiney baby to you for complaining," Lance whispered.

"No, not at all, Lance," I answered. "Every transition is rough; we all break and scream, cry, and yell. There's no shame in that given what your body is going through."

Another wave of pain hit him just then. He reached out and took my hand, squeezing it as hard as his he could. I wrapped both my hands around his one, talking gently to him until the pain passed. When it did, he simply smiled at me before slipping into sleep. I sighed, knowing he couldn't sleep through the whole thing, but grateful he was sleeping as long as he could.

While he was out for the moment I made sure the supplies we would need were all there. When I was satisfied they were I sat back down in the chair and got ready to be there for the long haul. Deciding there wasn't much I could do for him right then, I shut my eyes and took a nap until the next wave of pain hit him.

CHAPTER 3

It was well after two in the morning before I got to my room and crashed. Lance had survived his transition and was now sleeping in the infirmary. After the transition was complete, new vampires were fed as much blood as they could take and then put into a medically induced coma for a few days. While the worst was over, they would feel continual muscle cramps and spasms throughout their body. It was better for everyone if they got to sleep through that particular experience.

After catching about four hours of sleep I woke up knowing there was no way I was getting back to bed. The whole time I sat with Lance I'd thought about what Dimitri and Alexander said to me. As I sat there I'd made the decision to talk to Nate, and all I had wanted to do was find him. Instead, I waited until Lance was done and then went straight to sleep. It wouldn't make a lick of difference to the situation if I went to find Nate when I was too tired to think straight.

Now that I was somewhat rested I got up and headed towards his room. Nate and Lance shared a dorm room, so I knew Nate would be alone right now. What we needed to discuss was private, so I figured that right now while Lance was in the infirmary was the best time.

When I got to his room, I didn't bother knocking. Instead I entered the room and closed the door behind me. Nate must have had a rough night; he was sprawled out in the middle of the bed, blankets and sheets twisted together and thrown on the floor. Even looking at him now, I was struck by how handsome he was.

Nate was several inches shorter than my six-four. His wavy, light blond hair reached his ears, and although his eyes were closed, I knew them to be a deep forest green. It had been his soulful eyes that originally drew me to him. Even at his pre-trans height of about five-nine he had nicely toned, lean muscles. Looking at him now, I would guess he was about one seventy-five or so.

"Nate, wake up, we need to talk," I said as I leaned over and shook his shoulder. When he swatted my hand away in his sleep and rolled over, I smiled and sat on the bed. This time I grabbed his shoulder a little firmer and tried again. "Wake up, sleepy head."

"Matteo," he whispered after he turned and looked up at me. "I always have this dream."

Before I could ask what he was talking about, he reached up, locked his hands behind my neck, and pulled me down. I was so shocked at what was happening I didn't have time to react before his lips found mine. But when the sweet taste of Nate hit me, I fell into that kiss. Licking across his lips, Nate moaned and opened up his mouth for my searching tongue. It wasn't until he reached down and grabbed my now hard cock that I snapped out of my lust.

"Wait, this isn't why I came here," I said as I pushed away from him.

"Oh my god, I thought it was a dream," Nate whispered, turning several shades of red.

"It's okay, Nate."

"Why are you here, Matteo?" he asked, turning from embarrassed to pissed. "You made your feelings very clear last time we saw each other."

"No, I really didn't," I answered shaking my head, "I tried to push you away. And for that, and the hurt I caused you, I'm so sorry, Nate."

"What are you talking about?"

I took a deep breath and tried to collect myself before trying to explain. "It wasn't a mistake being with you, Nate. The only mistake was not waiting until after your transition."

"I'm so lost," he whispered as he ran his hands over his face. "What does my transition have to do with how we feel about each other?"

"Look, I'm telling you this as somebody who's been through their transition," I answered with a sigh. "I've also witnessed hundreds of transitions over the years, so I know what I'm talking about. I think we can both agree to that, right?"

Nate didn't say anything, but simply searched my face for a few moments. When he nodded, I continued my train of thought.

"People change after their transition, and I'm not just talking physically. It's more than a structural and bodily change, Nate. It can be emotional as well as mental."

"I guess I can see that," he replied. I could almost see the wheels spinning in his head as he thought about what I said. "So you're saying I might not feel the same about you, or us, after my transition."

"Yes," I whispered as he voiced my worst fear. I didn't know if my heart could take him not wanting me after his transition. "It wasn't just my feeling that it was wrong for me to touch a student keeping me away from you. I'm not saying you're too young to know what you want, Nate. It's more than that. You might be a totally different person after you transition."

"Why didn't you just say that?" he asked gently. I couldn't answer at first, and tried to turn away from his knowing, gorgeous eyes. But when he reached out and touched my cheek, I sucked it up and looked at him.

"Because I'm an ass," I answered honestly. "I've never really had sex with anyone I cared about before. And the idea that you might turn away from me after your transition because you don't want me anymore... well, it was too painful to really even think about."

"So, in reality, it had nothing to do with me but it was all about you."

"No, that's not what I'm saying," I replied, shaking my head. "I'm not explaining this right. Your birthday is in a couple of weeks. Why start something if we don't know if you'll feel the same after it?"

"Okay, that I get," he said, taking my hand. "But it's more than that, isn't it?"

"Yeah, it is. And I didn't realize it until I sat up with Lance during his transition," I replied, taking a few moments to gather myself again. "He asked about my transition and it brought up so many painful memories. I was invisible growing up, unless there was something for someone to yell at me, or blame me for. I could have died during my transition because my family didn't even care enough to tend to me or make sure I had blood at the right time."

The whole time I was talking, Nate was holding my hand tightly while rubbing his other hand over it. "How did you survive?"

"A warrior named Renaldo came to the house as I finished my transition," I explained. "My parents sent for him when it started, knowing I was going to be a warrior. Hell, I didn't even know anything about the transition, much less that I was a warrior. He got me out of there fast and made sure I got the blood I needed. Then he explained everything to me as we rode to the warrior camp in Spain."

"I do love your accent," Nate said as he leaned forward and placed a gentle kiss on my lips. "It gets me hard every time I hear it."

"Oh fuck, Nate," I groaned. "Please don't say things like that, you're going to kill me."

"I want you, Matteo."

"I can't," I whispered, blinking away the tears starting to burn my eyes. "I care too much about you already, if you change your mind about me after your transition it would be the death of me. I can't be tossed aside again, I wouldn't make it."

"I wouldn't do that—"

"You can't know that," I interrupted.

"What about after my transition? If I still feel the same will you be with me then?"

I searched his eyes, looking for a way to explain it was more than the transition. "I have a feeling that if we started something, even after your change, it would be serious. Are you sure you could give up playing the field and sowing your wild oats?"

"I don't care about any of that," he replied, shaking his head. "If I do after my transition, I will tell you. But if I feel the same as I do now, all I want is you, Matteo."

"Alright, we can talk again after your transition," I answered before letting go of his hands and standing. "I'm sorry I handled all of this so badly, I hope you can find it in your heart to forgive me."

"Now that I understand better, I do forgive you."

"Thanks, Nate," I said, opening the door. After a moment's hesitation, I turned back to look at him. "You really are a fine man."

I left then, closing the door behind me before he could say anything. As I headed back to my room I felt like a weight had been lifted off my shoulders. Granted it had been very hard for me to admit all that to Nate, but it seemed to have been the right thing to do. Not that I ever doubted Nate would understand; he was one of the best men I had met throughout my centuries of life.

When I reached my room I felt so tired that I was, once again, forever grateful I had the day off. Since I was in charge of overseeing every transition at the camp, Alexander and Dimitri always scheduled me to have a free day after each one. They said it was only fair after going through, and watching, something so emotional and trying. At first I had objected, not wanting to give up my duties training the newly post-transition warriors.

But after overseeing the first few transitions I realized it was a smart move on their part. Granted, I wasn't the one actually going through the transition, but it was still incredibly taxing on my nerves and emotionally exhausting. Crawling into bed, I felt better about life. As it was, I knew I would get hurt if Nate didn't want me after his transition. But the idea of me hurting him ate at my insides more.

As I started to drift off I wondered what Nate would look like after his transition. He would still have the same hair and eyes, of course. But would he be taller than me? How would it feel to have sex with him afterwards? Would he even let me top him after his transition? All these questions circled in my head as I fell asleep

* * * *

A few days later I was heading to Nate and Lance's room to check on how Lance was doing now that he was out of the infirmary. We didn't start his post-trans training program until tomorrow but I was praying for him to have changed into a better man with his new body.

"I said no!" I heard Nate yell from down the hall. Without even thinking, I took off as fast I could.

"I figure this is why everyone loves you, they've had a taste of this sweet ass," Lance said as I kicked down the door. What I saw in front of me is the only excuse I have for the way I reacted. Lance, with his new bigger build, had Nate pinned down over the desk while holding his hands behind his back. Nate's pants were ripped off of him and pooled around his ankles.

His attacker was trying to keep Nate still as he struggled, while lining up his cock with Nate's unprepared hole. I grabbed Lance around the throat and threw him across the room. Without even thinking of the new post-trans I knelt down next to Nate and pulled him into my arms.

"Nate, are you okay?" I asked in a whisper. The way his entire body shook, I knew he was far from okay. "Did I get here in time?"

"Yeah, you made it," he cried as he turned to hug me. The force of his lunge was so strong that I landed on my ass. In an instant, Nate straddled my lap and wrapped his arms and legs around me.

"He wanted it," Lance spat out as he wiped the blood off his face. It seemed that when I threw him, he slammed into the mirror hanging over the dresser. That worked for me. I couldn't have planned it better if I'd tried.

"Yeah, I can tell exactly how much he wanted it," I snarled at Lance as I held Nate tighter. "You just made the biggest mistake of your life, Lance. I challenge you. Tomorrow before breakfast, meet me at the circle."

The circle was preserved from the days of old. It was more like a fighting pit where challenges and the subsequent aftermath were held. It was only about five feet deep, but it allowed spectators the opportunity to get a first-hand view of what was going on while keeping them at a safe distance and preventing them from possibly interfering.

"You can't do that," he replied, visibly paling.

"Oh yes I can," I sneered. I felt a smile start to come over my face, and it wasn't a nice one. "Welcome to your post-transition, Lance, where the consequences of your actions are more severe."

"Fuck you, Matteo," he said as he stood and tried to gather himself.

"No, I'll be fucking you tomorrow, unless you're too chicken-shit to show," I replied. "Now get the fuck out of here before I snap and just kill you for touching him."

"What is it about this piece of shit that everyone adores?" Lance asked, shaking with rage. "Why the fuck is he so perfect to you all?"

"Get out, Lance. I won't warn you again," I growled, holding a still shaking Nate tightly in my arms. He must have realized how close I really was to snapping, because Lance turned without another word and stormed out of the room. "It's okay, Nate. I'm here, he can't hurt you anymore."

"Don't challenge him because of this," he whispered into my neck. "Then everyone will know what he tried to do to me."

"Yeah, but he didn't, baby," I soothed as I ran my hands up and down his back. "They need to know what kind of person he is. Plus letting this go unpunished is just a green light for him to try it again. Next time it might not be on you, and his victim will probably not have someone there to stop him."

"Okay," he said reluctantly, nodding. We didn't say anything for a while, simply sitting there in silence while I comforted him. When he finally stopped shaking, I stood with him in my arms before tucking him into bed.

"Will you stay with me?" Nate asked as I turned to leave. "Please, Matteo, I don't want to be alone."

"Just let me make a quick call out in the hallway, and then I'm all yours."

He looked me over for a minute, then simply nodded and closed his eyes. I watched him for a bit before stepping into the hallway and calling Dimitri.

"What's up, Matteo?" He asked before I could even say hello.

"I was coming to check on Lance before his new training schedule starts tomorrow," I said, trying desperately to control my rage. I knew my words were coming out clipped and that Dimitri could tell I was seething. "I heard Nate scream from down the hall and busted down the door just in time to stop Lance from shoving his dick into an unwilling Nate."

"That little motherfucker," Dimitri snarled. "Is he even alive?"

"Yeah, he's fine," I replied, then started chuckling. "I grabbed him and threw him across the room. He'll be picking bits of mirror out of his skin. Hopefully it will heal before he gets them all, then he'll have to cut himself back open and dig them out."

"That's it? You threw him off Nate? How did you control yourself like that?" Dimitri asked, amazement apparent in his voice.

"All that mattered was comforting Nate," I said quietly, hoping he couldn't hear me through the door. "I've never seen anyone shake like that, Dimitri. It broke my heart."

"Good point. I'm still not sure I wouldn't have killed him, but I feel you."

"I did challenge him tomorrow morning," I answered, starting to squirm. It wasn't unheard of for a warrior to challenge a post-trans vampire, but it was more common between warriors. Lance had months of training ahead of him before he could even start to be considered for that. I wasn't hopeful for a positive response about it from Dimitri.

"Kick the fucker's ass, dude," Dimitri said, almost causing me to drop the phone in surprise. "Maybe it will bring him down a few pegs."

"That so is not the response I was expecting," I replied as I burst out laughing. "I thought I'd get some kind of lecture."

"Nope, not from me. I'd have killed the little bastard."

"Okay, good to know," I snickered. "Look, can you get someone to cover for me today? I want to be here for Nate."

"You got it, brother. Take care of your boy," Dimitri said, hanging up the phone before I could correct him. Shaking my head, I turned and went back into Nate's room. He was lying in the bed, just watching me, as tears streamed down his face.

"Oh, don't cry, baby," I said as I toed off my shoes before crawling into bed with him. "I talked to Dimitri; he's got my training covered. I'm here for you all day."

"Thanks, Matteo," he whispered as he pulled my arm tighter around him. We didn't say anything else for hours. I wasn't going to try and make him talk. What do you say to someone who went through what Nate just did? I didn't know, but risking saying the wrong thing wasn't something I was willing to do.

* * * *

The next morning I stood in the challenge circle, stretching out and waiting for my opponent to arrive. We had a bet going between most of the warriors who worked in training; whether Lance would even show or not. Lance didn't have to accept my challenge. Normally honor drove a warrior to do it, but we all knew the little —or I guess not so little anymore— shit didn't have any of that.

Dimitri had already contacted the council and brought Lance up on attempted rape charges. While the council always took that kind of thing seriously, the fact Lance tried to rape a pre-trans was a huge deal. A warrior's main job was to protect those who couldn't protect themselves. Going against one of our main mottos, and trying to force himself on Nate, was right up there with slaughtering a council member.

If Lance weren't from such a well-connected family, he'd already be in our prison waiting for the council's decision. In my mind, this worked out better because I couldn't have challenged him from behind bars.

"This is going to be fun," Lance said loudly as he jumped down into the circle.

"I can't believe you had the balls to show," I replied, not reacting to his idea of a grand entrance. "You do realize what happens when I win, right?"

"You won't win, Matteo," he snickered. I didn't even have a chance to respond before the dozens of warriors gathered started to laugh.

"Oh yeah, Matteo is fourth in rank because he sucks," Yuri laughed. Yuri was actually third in rank behind Dimitri and Alexander. While I took my position —and being a warrior— seriously, I was cool with those who were ahead of me in rank. That's why I never even tried to challenge them. I liked leading, and being towards the top, I just never felt the drive to be number one; being the best also came with a slew of responsibilities I just didn't want.

"Is that an option for when he loses?" Lance asked as he turned towards Yuri. "I think I'd prefer him sucking my cock on his knees than being in his ass."

Lance's bravado faltered slightly when we all started laughing that time. It wasn't just some chuckles; everyone there was gripping their stomachs in full belly laughs. To have this brand new, post-trans vampire acting all badass when he was about to fight a centuries-old warrior was just too funny for words.

I knew Lance thought he had an ace up his sleeve. While pre-trans weren't trained on how to use swords, some older warrior families taught their children before they came to camp. Lance was one of those children; he'd been working with swords and various weapons since he was in his teens. And to a cocky shit like him, he thought the home training made him all that. Even though the idiot believed it, the rest of us knew it didn't mean shit next to all the years under my belt.

"Do I get Nate, too, after I win?" Lance asked as we moved into position.

"The charges you're facing have nothing to do with this challenge," Alexander answered as he crossed his arms over his chest. "And the only one who can give Nate away is Nate."

"I just liked seeing Matteo's reaction," Lance snickered. I took a deep breath, knowing he was trying to get me to fight while enraged. That was the quickest way to make mistakes in any fight. I was smart enough, and experienced enough, to see that.

"You'll be seeing all kinds of reactions from me," I answered with a knowing smirk. Lance paled again before recovering his demeanor.

We moved into position, giving each other the normal salute. We faced each other, the normal ten feet apart, with our swords held at an angle so the top of the weapon hit our left shoulder. We both bowed ceremoniously, out of respect to each other and the fight to come. In a flash we were both in fighting stances, swords raised over head, elbows and knees slightly bent.

Normally I took a more defensive fight position while I learned my opponent's tactics. But fighting someone like Lance, who I'd helped train over the past year, I already knew his weaknesses. I swung overhead lightning quick, making Lance raise his sword to block me. However, since I moved first and startled him, he couldn't stop the full force of my swing. His sword went back far enough to slice a small part of his cheek.

It was then I realized how scared Lance truly was. Not waiting for him to recover, I spun to my right while striking out to his side. Knowing he was right-handed and would lead his defense that way, attacking his left side kept him at a disadvantage. He swiped at my sword weakly as he turned and tried to get out of my way; instead I was able to nick his left shoulder.

When I moved towards him, he feebly tried to thrust his sword at my chest, which was exactly what I had hoped he would do. Striking hard at his sword from his right, he had to compensate with his left. He cried out in pain as his now injured left shoulder failed him and he dropped his sword.

"Kneel and admit defeat," I growled as I stepped closer with the blade of my sword now pointed at his throat. He swallowed loudly and tried to hide his glance at his sword on the ground. "You'll never make it, Lance. Yield and I'll let you live."

His eyes bulged out of his head then, seemingly shocked at my words. I doubted anyone had ever not let Lance slide before, but after the shit he pulled he was lucky I didn't kill him. Part of it was the glimpse I got into the real Lance during his transition. I really hoped his defeat and humiliation would knock him down a few levels and maybe help make him into the man I knew he could be.

"I yield," he said quietly as he dropped to his knees with his head hanging down in shame.

"Maybe I should just fuck your face instead of your ass, like you wanted to do to me?" I whispered in his ear as I tossed my sword off to the side. Moving behind him, I pushed Lance down onto his hands and knees, knowing it would be painful with his injury. As our audience got quiet, I reached over and ripped Lance's shirt and shorts off him. I had to admit, he was stunning. But this wasn't about having sex for fun.

I pulled my own shirt off and knelt behind Lance. Looking up at Dimitri, I nodded. We'd decided beforehand that this was about Lance realizing he wasn't as powerful and untouchable as he thought he was. But at the same time, I didn't want to cause him unnecessary pain. Dimitri tossed me a bottle of lube which I caught with ease. While Lance had to submit to me, I wasn't looking to tear his ass up.

Squirting some lube onto my fingers, I pushed two into Lance's tight hole. He cried out and his body started to shake under my touch. I didn't love the idea of doing this in front of people, I'd never been an exhibitionist, but it was part of Lance's humiliation. I knew starting with two fingers would give Lance a bit of pain; I said I wouldn't rip his ass up, not make sure it was purely pleasurable for him.

When I could move two fingers around inside Lance, I shoved in a third. He screamed, but didn't really sound like he was in pain. Looking under Lance, I could see his cock was rock hard. It hit me then that he seemed to be putting on a show that he didn't want this for the other warriors.

"Was this your plan all along, Lance?" I whispered as I shoved all three fingers into his ass hard.

"No, this isn't how I wanted it," he mumbled. Annoyed, I got even rougher with him before he continued. "When I heard Nate talking in his sleep about being with you in the showers, I knew it wasn't just a dream."

"So you decided to rape him?" I asked in astonishment, not seeing where this conversation was heading.

"I'm not sure I would even have done it," Lance answered as he looked over his shoulder at me. "I just got so pissed off. Why him and not me? What is it about Nate that everyone fawns all over him and loves him so?"

"For one, no matter how upset he was at anyone, he would never have even thought to rape them," I ground out to remind him, and myself, how we got there. "This isn't for your enjoyment, Lance. This is supposed to humiliate and humble you."

"Believe me, I'm humiliated," he said turning back away from me. "This isn't what I ever pictured when I dreamed of being with you."

That got me to freeze, completely shocked. After a few moments and a couple of deep breaths, I pulled my fingers out of his ass. A large part of me wanted to stop this right then, a small part of me was flattered that Lance wanted me. But it would have gone against the whole point of this to have stopped then, no matter if I'd lost part of my anger at him. He still needed to be taught a lesson for his actions.

I lined up my now lubed cock with Lance's tight hole. Not holding back, I slammed in all the way to the hilt in one shot. Lance's whole body shivered as he let out a loud groan.

"That's it, fuck that tight ass into submission," someone yelled out from the group.

If my head hadn't already been spinning out of control with the new development to this situation, I might have been able to better focus on my surroundings. As it was, I easily blocked out most of the cheering and catcalls. I heard all of them; they just didn't seem to register with my brain right then.

Lance's body was so tight around my hard cock it made me think back to being with Nate in the showers. I closed my eyes and dreamed I was back there instead of fucking the troublemaker under me with several dozen warriors watching. Pulling back out until just the head of my cock was still in him, I thrust back in as hard as I could. Reaching forward, I grabbed onto Lance's shoulders to get better leverage.

I pounded into his ass like I've never fucked anyone before. Still pretending it was the man I loved under me, I enjoyed it much more than I would have thought. It was easy to see Lance had very few, if anyone, ever fuck him. Pistoning my hips even faster, I felt my balls start to draw up. I cried out loudly as I came, opening my eyes when I heard someone else cry out.

Nate was standing in the front of the group, his eyes glued on me. I was still thrusting in and out of Lance's ass when our eyes locked. Before I could even call out to him, he turned and pushed his way through the crowd. I was still shaking from my orgasm when I heard Lance grunt loudly before his ass clamped down on my softening cock.

Looking down I saw him shoot his load all over the ground. I leaned over and hissed in his ear, "You weren't supposed to have enjoyed this, Lance. If I ever see or hear of you touching someone who doesn't want it again, I will kill you."

"It won't ever happen again," he panted just before he collapsed on ground muddy with his seed. "I've learned my lesson; I just couldn't control my rage. I swear I'll figure out a way to handle my anger. Please just promise me that you'll fuck me again, without everyone watching this time?"

"Not going to happen," I answered in disgust as I pulled up my shorts. Lance had a content smile on his face and while I knew it embarrassed him to be taken this way, it was apparent how much he enjoyed it. I shook my head, not sure how I felt about all of this as I retrieved my shirt.

"What about him?" Dimitri asked me, gesturing over to Lance as I climbed up out of the circle.

"Take him to the holding cell, I guess," I answered with a deep sigh. "We need to talk about this later, but for now, I need to go after Nate."

"He was here?" Alexander asked, shock written all over his face. I tried to ignore the way he was touching my best friend. Rolling my eyes at the fact my supposed punishment of Lance was going to help Dimitri's sex life, I simply nodded and broke through the crowd. I ran as fast as I could on shaky legs towards Nate's room. I just hoped that he would give me a chance to explain.

CHAPTER 4

"Nate, please open up," I called out as I pounded on his door.

"Go away," he sobbed. It broke my heart to know he'd been crying. And what was worse, I was the one to have made him cry. Again.

"Can't do it. Let me in or I'm going to break down the door."

Without a word, Nate opened the door and walked back to the bed. He threw himself face down on the mattress, still sobbing. I watched, feeling helpless as his entire body shook with the force of his cries. Closing the door behind me, I turned and went over the bed.

"Please, talk to me," I said as I sat on the bed. When he didn't say anything I leaned over and started rubbing his back.

"Don't touch me," he yelled as he pulled away from me. That really hurt. I watched in horror as he moved to the far corner of the bed, up against the wall. "I can't believe you would come to me still smelling like that asshole."

"I'm sorry, Nate," I replied, running my fingers through my hair in frustration. "I wasn't thinking about any of that. I saw your face and all I could think about was getting to you."

"You enjoyed it," Nate spat out, not as a question, but an accusation.

"Only because I was picturing being with you, baby."

"*He* enjoyed it."

"I didn't realize that until after I saw you," I replied, nodding. "But I also talked to him, and he hadn't meant to do what he did to you. Lance swore he didn't think he was even going to rape you."

Nate just sat there, staring at me with his mouth wide open, "And you believe him?"

"I think so," I answered with a shrug. "Lance said he heard you talking in your sleep about us being together in the showers. It seems he's had a crush on me and got jealous and filled with rage. I'm not excusing what he did, Nate. I'm just saying, right after the transition it's really hard to control your emotions. So, while I'm not a hundred percent sure I believe him, his story does have merit."

"And I can't understand because I've not been through my transition, is that right?"

"I'm not saying that," I said, trying to choose my words carefully. "Maybe you've had a sudden onslaught of emotions at one time or another, where you can understand losing it. That's what it feels like for weeks after your transition."

Nate sat back against the wall, seeming to ponder over what I just said. "That doesn't make it right."

"No, it doesn't. But I thought you would want to know that it wasn't something he planned, or maybe didn't even really realize he was doing it. Isn't that better for you to know, rather than think he set out to hurt you?"

"You're right," he said quietly as he nodded his head. "But I thought fucking him after he lost was supposed to be some humiliating experience? What I saw was two people having enjoyable sex while a bunch of voyeurs watched."

"It is supposed to demean him, it just didn't work out that way. Fuck," I grumbled, "I didn't know what to do when he told me he wanted me. I mean I was already stretching him out, everyone was watching. This was supposed to be a message to him and to others that this kind of shit can't be tolerated. If I had stopped there, it would have been like excusing his behavior."

"I get that you were in a tough spot, but that doesn't mean I have to like it."

"I wouldn't expect you to," I answered truthfully. "If the tables were turned, I'd be seething. But I'm telling you the truth, Nate. I wouldn't lie to you."

"I believe that," he answered, still searching my face. "But it still hurts to look at you right now. Can you please just leave me alone for now while I think?"

"Okay, baby," I said as my head hung down in defeat. For some reason, knowing that looking at me hurt him, I couldn't seem to look at him either. Without another word I left the room. Instead of going back to my room I headed to Dimitri's office.

Even though I was pretty sure my friend was currently getting lucky, I didn't really have anywhere else to be. On the way, I glanced over to the now empty circle and shuddered. How could I have been so blind as to how Lance felt? I mean, there hadn't been any outward signs he liked me, but looking back I had to admit that I was the only instructor he didn't give a hard time to.

I was surprised when I got to Dimitri's office and he was there… making out with his mate like a teenager. Needing a good laugh, I entered the open door and plopped down in one of the chairs to watch. For several moments I just sat there, watching as Alexander and Dimitri continued on, completely oblivious.

"Can you turn a little so I can get a better view?" I asked, just to be a shit.

"Get out," Alexander growled, not even looking up from where he was kissing my best friend's neck.

"Hey, you watched me earlier, tit for tat, my friend," I chuckled.

"Never took you for a voyeur," Dimitri moaned. "Now get

out."

"We really do need to talk about what I learned, Dimitri."

"Fine," he grumbled as he pulled away from Alexander. I laughed as I saw that they both had raging hard-ons. Dimitri sat in his chair and pulled Alexander down onto his lap. "Talk fast. I want to pound my cock into my mate's ass."

"I was thinking the same thing, except my cock in your ass," Alexander purred as he wiggled on Dimitri's lap. "You were in my ass last."

"Alright guys, I started the joke," I said, putting my hands over my eyes as if to block what I was seeing in my head. "But you're taking it too far. No mental images please."

"Fine, tell us about Lance," Dimitri replied, running his hands up and down Alexander's arms. "Did I see wrong, or was he enjoying himself?"

"He wasn't happy about the setting, but it seems he's wanted to be with me for a while now," I said. Then I explained everything Lance told me about Nate, what had happened, and his rage. "I guess I'm just that irresistible."

"Yeah, yeah, you're a Spanish god," Dimitri chuckled. "Do you think he got the punishment?"

"To a point, but not like we thought he would," I answered as I leaned back over the chair to stretch out. All the stress had my muscles feeling tight. "So what do we do from here?"

"Well, he's in lock-up," Alexander replied. I wondered if I should tell them that, as subtle as they were trying to be, I still saw Dimitri's hand playing with Alexander's dick in his pants. "I can understand uncontrollable rage so shortly after someone's transition, but Lance has been a thorn in everyone's ass since he got here."

"Yeah, but have you ever met the kid's parents? It's a wonder he's not a mass murderer," I answered. "Look, I'm not trying to make excuses for Lance. What he did was wrong. But I also think he knows that, and the farther away we get him from his asshole parents, the larger a chance he has to grow into a fine warrior."

"You want that task?" Dimitri asked raising an eyebrow. "I'm not suggesting you exploit his feelings for you, but you've gotten through to him. You cared enough to be there for him during his transition when his parents weren't."

"Fine, I'll try, but I'm not making any promises," I said reluctantly.

"Good, now get out of here so I can fuck my mate," Alexander said, then moaned.

I chuckled but looked away; I didn't need to see what Dimitri did to make him moan. "Glad I could help your sex life."

"Don't kid yourself, brother," Dimitri snickered as he took off his shirt. "Our sex life is off the charts awesome, we didn't need any help."

I didn't respond, simply walked out of the office and closed the door behind me. Walking back towards my rooms I realized I had a lot of thinking to do; not only about this whole Lance thing, but also Nate, and my feelings with everything that had happened.

* * * *

A week later, Nate was still avoiding me like the plague. He wouldn't talk to me, and wouldn't answer when I spoke to him unless it was in my role as an instructor. The only good thing that happened during the week was that I seemed to be getting through to Lance. Once he saw that even though I didn't return his feelings, I did care for him, his old asshole ways seemed to disappear. It wasn't an overnight transformation, but it was progressive.

"Okay, I think that's enough for the day," I called out to Lance when I saw he was dragging through the drills I had him running.

"Matteo, you need to come with me, right now," Yuri yelled as he sprinted towards us.

"What's wrong?"

"It's Nate, he's gone into his transition almost a week early," he panted as he stopped and tried to catch his breath. At first I just stared at Yuri as if he'd told me I was royalty, frozen where I was standing. Then it was like something snapped inside me and without another thought I took off like a flash towards the infirmary. I heard Yuri and Lance running behind me but I put everything I had into my steps. Since I had always been pretty fast, even by vampire standards, neither of them could keep up with me.

I busted through the doors of the infirmary, then the trauma room, and skidded to a stop. Nate lay on one of the beds, writhing in pain. Just then he screamed so loudly that I was surprised the windows in the room hadn't broken.

"I'm here, Nate," I said as I ran to his bed. Reaching down I took his hands in mine and let him squeeze as hard as he could. "Just breathe, baby. Nice, deep breaths."

"Matteo," he hissed out, the pain written all over his face. "What's wrong? Why am I early?"

"I don't know, Nate," I answered before looking up at the doctors. "Has anyone contacted his parents?"

"No, he was just brought in a few minutes ago," one of them answered before walking away.

"Nate, I'm going to go call your parents, okay?"

"Just need you here," he whimpered. Then he screamed out in pain again.

"I know, baby, I'm here. But I have to call them," I replied, kissing his forehead. He let go of my hands and nodded. As much as it killed me to leave him just then, I knew it had to be done. Plus, maybe his parents could shed some light on why Nate was going thought his transition early. I pulled Nate's file as I left the main room and dialed the number to reach his parents.

"Hello?"

"Mr. Hathus? This is Matteo Dominguez," I said evenly.

"Nate? Oh my god, is he okay?"

"He's going through his transition, sir."

"Already? How is that possible?" he asked me.

"I was hoping you could tell me that, Mr. Hathus. It's important that I know about you and your wife's transition," I explained to him. "A parent's transition can tell us a lot about what to expect."

"Well, umm, hold on, Matteo." I heard muffled talking in the background. My eyebrows drew together in confusion, why was that such a difficult question?

"Look, there's something I need to tell you, but Nate doesn't know," Mr. Hathus said when he got back on the phone. "Nate was adopted."

"We don't have that in our records," I said feeling the anger start to rise in me. "Don't you think the people looking after your son and his transition would need to know that?"

"We've never told anyone and we didn't see how you knowing he was adopted would matter."

"It does," I growled trying to stay calm. "Are you sure

whomever you adopted him from told you his correct birthday?"

"Well, that's the thing," Mr. Hathus said, sighing into the phone. "My wife can't conceive children, so when Nate was left as an orphan a friend of ours brought him to us. We accepted him with open arms, grateful for the chance to have a child. But he was already almost a year old at the time. They told us his birth date and whatnot, but as you know, there isn't a way to verify such information."

"So you were basically guessing and didn't bother to tell us this?" I snarled, fully pissed off at this time. "And he doesn't know this. Great! Just fucking great."

"We thought it was best he didn't know," Mr. Hathus started to explain, but I cut him off.

"Fine, at least we know why he's gone into his transition early. I need to go tend to him," I said not looking forward to the hours ahead. "I'm going to have to tell him, he's scared shitless something is wrong."

"You can't tell him, he'll never forgive us," he gasped.

"Letting him think he might be dying is better?"

"Well, no…"

"I'll figure something out, but I'm not going to hide it from him like you did," I grumbled into the phone, then hung up before he could respond. I knew it was childish, but really, I just didn't have the time or energy to fight with Nate's dad just then. Taking a few deep breaths and collecting myself before going back in the other room, I realized that when I saw Nate, I couldn't lie to him.

"Nate, I got the answer," I said gently as I reached him. "It's okay that you're going into your transition now. I promise."

"Why is this happening to me?" he asked, panting. The pain had subsided for the moment, and he looked so wiped. "Am I going to make it?"

"You'll be fine, baby," I answered stroking his cheek. "I'll explain everything to you later, but it really is okay."

"Please, just tell me now."

"I can't do that, Nate. Right now you need to focus on what's happening."

"Please, Matteo?" he asked, tears forming in his eyes, "I'm scared and I need to know why this is happening early." Nate looked freaked out, and if he didn't calm down soon, his transition would be worse.

I leaned over and kissed his sweet, soft lips. "Your father just told me that you're adopted. Your birth parents died when you were about one year old, and while they thought they knew your real birthday, it's possible they were wrong. They didn't know your birth parents personally, and a friend of theirs brought you to them knowing they couldn't have children of their own."

"What?" he gasped as he tried to pull away from me, but I wouldn't let him.

I took his face firmly in my hands and gave him another quick kiss. "You can deal with all of this later, baby, okay? I'll explain it again after you transition and we can go beat up your parents for keeping secrets. But please, please, Nate, I need you to push it aside and focus on your transition," I pleaded with him. "Right now you need to stay calm and just focus on your breathing. I need you to stay with me right now."

"Matteo, I can't just," he started to say, but then another wave of pain hit and he screamed.

"Did you give him the drugs?" I yelled over to the doctors.

"No, we didn't know what to do with him entering his transition early," one of them answered me.

"I talked with his parents, it's fine," I replied. "Help him, give him the drugs."

The man searched my face for a few moments before nodding and turning towards the table and working on a syringe.

"How could they lie to me like that?" Nate asked, starting to sob. "All these years, never telling me I was adopted. Why? Why would they do that to me?"

"Probably so you never had to feel like you do right now," I answered as I moved him to a sitting up position. I decided right then to do something I never did with vampires in their transition; I refused to stay detached. Crawling into bed behind him, I sat up, my back leaning against the wall. I moved Nate so that he was reclining up against my chest with his body in between my legs. I wrapped both arms around him, hugging him to me as gently as possible.

"Do you think they ever loved me?"

"I think they love you very much, Nate," I answered honestly. "I don't think there is ever a good time to have that kind of conversation with someone you love. And they see you as their son, so what did it ever matter that you weren't born from your mother?"

"I guess that makes sense," Nate replied, running his hands over my arms. "Does this change the way you feel about me?"

"Absolutely not," I said completely aghast. "I love you for the man you are, not your lineage or who your parents are."

"You love me?" he asked, turning to look in my eyes. Unable to answer at the moment, I simply nodded. "I love you too, Matteo."

"I hope you still do tomorrow," I whispered as I leaned down to give him another kiss. Nate broke the kiss to gasp in pain again. Just then the doctor came over and gave Nate a shot in his arm. It seemed to help, smoothing away the lines of pain and stress on his gorgeous face.

"Just rest, Nate. You'll need your strength to get through this."

"Will you stay with me?" he asked as he turned to the side to curl up. I moved my arms so that he could adjust his position; his head on my shoulder and his legs thrown over one of my thighs. He was still in between my legs, but more like if I was carrying him while I walked. Again, I gently wrapped my arms around him.

"I'm not going anywhere, Nate," I answered, laying my head on top of his. "Believe me, I'm feeling every painful twinge with you, baby. If I could bear this for you, I would."

"I know you would," Nate replied smiling up at me. "It's one of the reasons I fell in love with you. You have the biggest, softest heart. But don't worry, I won't tell anyone."

"Thanks, I have to keep up my street cred," I said chuckling. Nate giggled before gasping in pain again.

I sat there, helpless to help him, but trying to soothe him nonetheless. We didn't say anything as the minutes, and then hours, ticked by. While I watched Nate's suffering I felt my heart breaking as I desperately wanted to help him. I knew they were hopeless wishes, but they were ones I couldn't stop myself from making.

CHAPTER 5

I woke up from my nap to Nate's screams. I held on to him as gently as I could, praying to the powers that be for this to end soon. Thankfully he was through most of his transition, but now he was experiencing skull-splitting pain as his fangs grew in. I felt hot tears streaming down my face as I tried to lend him every ounce of my strength.

"You're almost done, baby," I whispered in his ear as it seemed the pain started to subside. When I felt him finally go slack against me, I knew he was finally done. Looking down at the now large man in my arms, I started to wonder if the small hospital bed we were in would be able to hold us up.

I moved out from behind him and grabbed the bags of blood. Reaching out to help him sit up again, I lifted the first bag towards his face.

"No," he whispered, "I won't drink it."

"Baby, your fangs are in now," I replied completely confused. "It's time for you to drink. You made it."

"But look how big I am."

"What does that have to do with anything?" I asked, not following his train of thought.

"I'm not the little Nate you fell for anymore," he whimpered as tears streamed down his face. "You're not going to want me anymore."

"Baby, that's not true," I answered sitting down on the bed in front of him. "You're still gorgeous, just in a different way. Inside, I know you'll still be the man I fell in love with."

"You don't know that," he sobbed, clutching onto my shirt.

"I don't know that, but I feel it in my heart," I answered, taking his hands into mine. "Your emotions are running all over the place, Nate. You've been through hell and back, just give yourself time to adjust to it."

"No… no… I know you won't want me," Nate replied, still crying loudly. "I won't survive your rejection of me. I won't drink the blood. Just please, let me die."

"Not a fucking chance," I growled, taking his head into my hands. "I didn't just suffer through this with you to let you die now. I want you, Nate. I just need to know that you want me once things settle down."

"You're just saying that so I'll drink." How could a vampire that big sound sulky?

"I've never once lied to you, baby, I'm not going to start now. Now drink the blood, Nate. It's important you do it now."

"No, I won't drink from the bag," he answered pulling away from me.

"From the bag? What will you drink from?"

"You," he replied, looking straight into my eyes. "If you love me, and you're so sure I won't change, then let me drink from you."

"Nate," I whispered, finally seeing what he was getting at. He wanted to mate with me to ensure I wouldn't ever leave him. "We need to wait, baby. You're too upset right now; we need to give it some time. Once we both calm down and adjust to the changes, we can talk about it."

"See, I knew you wouldn't want me when I'm huge like this," he said, pushing against my chest. Nate was right about one thing; he was huge. He had to have grown as big as Dimitri. I hadn't seen him stand up yet, but he was at least six-seven and three hundred pounds. I was large for a vampire and warrior, but even I felt a little scrawny sitting here with Nate.

"It's not that, Nate," I replied, shaking my head. "You're still every bit as breath-taking to me, but your emotions aren't under control."

Before he could even answer me, he turned to the side and threw up. Fuck! That meant his body needed the blood now. It would start eating his internal organs soon, then his muscles, until his body consumed itself if it didn't get the blood it craved.

"Baby, please, I don't want you to hate me later for giving in," I said, rubbing his back as he kept trying to push me away as he finished vomiting.

"If you loved me like you say you do, you wouldn't have to think twice about being mated to me," Nate cried. I knew he wasn't in his right mind; his body, hormones, and everything else were completely off-kilter. But seeing the pain in his eyes and after everything he went through, not just with the transition but learning of his adoption, I couldn't deny him.

I leaned in and kissed him gently on his lips before pulling back and tilting my head to the side. "I hope this is something you really want after you even out from your transition. Please, don't hate me for giving in, Nate."

"I won't, I love you," he answered as he leaned in to lick my neck. I felt my whole body shake at the sensation. Nate wrapped his arms around me and up my back, grabbing my hair in one hand and pulling me closer. Before I could even think about changing my mind he sank his fangs into my neck.

Instantly, my cock swelled, then erupted with the first suck he took of my blood. I moaned loudly reaching to stroke my cock through my running pants as my orgasm went on, wave after wave. After a few minutes Nate lifted his head up and licked the bite closed.

"I want in your sweet ass, Matteo," he whispered as he sucked on my ear. "I'm not sure if this is normal, but I've never, ever wanted or needed to be with someone like I do at this moment."

"I think it's because of the mating, not your transition."

"Please, let me fuck you, my mate," he begged, moving my hand over his rock solid cock. "I need to feel you."

"I've never had someone inside me before," I replied, completely unprepared for the turn of events.

"Good, then I'll have been the only one," Nate growled as he moved off the bed. "Just as you are the only one who's been in my ass."

"That seems fair," I whispered, still feeling the aftershocks of our mating and my orgasm.

"We don't have to do this if you don't want to," he said gently as he reached out and cupped my cheek.

I shook my head at first, trying to put my jumbled emotions into words. "It's not that I don't want to, I'm just on overload from the mating. And after centuries of sex I feel like a virgin again, since I've never let anyone take my ass."

"Oh god, you're killing me," Nate groaned as he rubbed his erection against my leg as it hung over the side of the bed. "I don't want to pressure you, Matteo. But fuck, I want to be in you so badly."

"Take me, my mate," I answered, still scared, but also excited about the idea of my mate's cock in me. I'd never wanted anyone to fuck me before; it was a new experience. And the wide, feral smile he gave me was worth my fear.

"Roll over," he growled as he ripped off his clothes.

I did as he asked. Before I could even move to take off my clothes Nate's hands were there taking them off me. Bent over the bed as I was, I couldn't see what he was doing, but I heard some items moving on the table. "Nate, can we do this so I can see you?" I asked hesitantly.

"Of course we can. I actually prefer that idea," he answered as he rubbed my ass. "Turn back over."

I gladly did, smiling up at him as I moved my hands under my thighs and pulled them to my chest. Nate growled deep in his chest before leaning over and licking my puckered hole. Fuck! I'd never had anyone lick me there before. It felt amazing. I watched as his head moved, and my cock started to harden again. When he pushed his tongue into my ass I let out a loud moan.

A few moments later, he removed his tongue and slipped in a lubed finger. Looking around I saw he hadn't used lube, but hand lotion. Hey, whatever worked. I let the sensation of Nate playing with my ass overtake me.

"Am I hurting you?" he asked as his eyes devoured my body.

"No, feels good," I panted. "More. I want more, Nate."

He smiled a sexy little smile at me that was all Nate; even with his new, larger body it was still the Nate I loved. Pushing another finger in gently, he started scissoring them around. I held on tighter to my legs as my body started to shake. When he pushed in a third finger I skated on the edge of control.

"Enough. Stick your cock in me already," I hissed, loving the feeling of being so full and the slight bite of pain. "Fuck me into the bed, baby."

"My pleasure," he answered, pulling his fingers out of me. Nate moved to line his cock up with my hole and started to push in. We both groaned loudly as he started to work about half of his cock in and out of me. Looking down, I saw that Nate's dick had grown to at least

ten or eleven inches. I was shocked my body could even take that
much.

"God, this feels fucking amazing," I moaned as he started to
push more of himself into me. With one hard thrust, he bottomed out in
my ass. Nate leaned down and kissed me, tongue thrusting right into
my mouth. I wrapped my arms around his neck as our tongues tangled.
Loving the full feeling of my mate being in me, I noticed he didn't
move while my body adjusted to his size. "And you thought I wouldn't
like the new, huge Nate."

"Stupid me," he chuckled as he moved my legs over his
shoulders and grabbed my hips. "I'm not sure of my new strength,
Matteo. I don't want to hurt you."

"You could never hurt me, Nate," I said. "Now fuck like
you've never fucked before."

Nate's eyes grew wide at my words as a look of pure lust and
desire crossed his face. Taking me at my word he started a hard and fast
rhythm. I reached over head and grabbed onto the side of the bed,
almost afraid he was going to push me off with his forceful thrusts.

"Getting close, Matteo," he grunted in between thrusts. I'd
never seen anything so beautiful as Nate was right at that moment. His
face was a combination of pure bliss and sensuality. Nate's large, strong
body showed the exertion he was putting forth. Every muscle moved
with him, showing off his new, sexy physique.

"Come for me, my mate," I panted as I reached down and took
my cock in my hand. I started stroking along it to the pace Nate was
fucking me.

"Shit, that's hot," he groaned, licking his lips as he looked
between my leaking cock and my face. "I love you so much, Matteo."

"I love you too, Nate," I cried out as my dick started spurting cum. I felt my ass tighten around his cock, as he roared. Even though I was pretty sure I'd never come so hard in my life, I kept stroking myself, extending my orgasm. "Fuck, so good!"

"So beautiful," Nate gasped before yelling out my name loudly. I felt him stiffen and watched the tendons in his neck bulge out seconds before I felt his seed fill my ass. He thrust several more times before collapsing on top of me.

"That was…" I panted, not even able to coherently finish my thought as we lay there shaking. I ran my hands up and down his back as we both tried to get our breathing under control. Nate's cock finally softened enough to slip out of my ass. It was another new experience for me, feeling his seed start to run out of my ass. Without thinking, I started laughing.

"What's so funny?" he asked lifting his head to look down at me.

"Your cum's running out my ass and it feels funny," I answered honestly. "That and I never thought I would ever have my ass fucked, and it was more amazing than I could ever have guessed."

"You don't regret it, do you?" The flicker of uncertainty on his face was apparent.

"Fuck no," I said taking his face in my hands. "I loved it, I love being with you. It was just as great as our time in the showers. With you I don't mind being the bottom as well as the top."

"Good, because I really liked it as well," he replied, smiling. Leaning over, he kissed my lips quickly before standing. "Now let's get you cleaned up."

"Nate, you need to lie down," I answered, shaking my head. "I can't believe you even were able to do that. Normally I'd be helping to put the post-transition into a coma, not allowing them any exertion like sex."

"I feel fine," he said, shrugging his shoulders as he reached for the box of tissues. Not my idea of how to clean up, but it would do given where we were. I wasn't able to move quickly enough as Nate dropped to his knees. "Actually, I change my answer, Matteo."

"I think you had an adrenaline and endorphin rush from the mating," I said, lifting him in my arms and then laying him down on a different, clean bed. "Now you're starting to feel what most post-trans feel after they've had blood."

"It's not as bad as before," he answered as he curled into a ball. "But, fuck, it still hurts."

"I'm going to put you under, baby," I said, running my fingers through his soft hair. "We can't put someone under during the transition, but it won't affect you if we do for the few days afterwards. You don't have to suffer through this part."

"No, it's okay. I can handle this," Nate said shaking his head.

"Not your call, Nate. It's procedure, you know that," I chuckled. "You don't get special favors because you're my mate. I have to do this. It won't just be a few hours of waves of pain. It will be a constant, dull pain everywhere. Please, I can't watch you suffer any more when I can help you now."

"Okay, Matteo," he replied quietly. "But only because it hurts you to see me like this."

"Quite noble of you, baby," I whispered against his lips before kissing him.

"I don't want to leave you, even for a few days," Nate said as I moved away to grab the necessary syringes. "We just mated, this should be our honeymoon period."

"It will be, sweetheart, just after you wake up," I assured him as I put the different meds into a bag of blood. Once that was done I turned to Nate and hooked him up to the IV. "Just go to sleep now, baby. You'll wake up and most of the pain will be past. Then we can see and explore all the new, fun things you can do with this hot body."

"Oh, fuck that sounds good," he moaned as his eyelids started to droop. Even though we combined the medicine with the blood, it was fast acting. "I love you, Matteo."

"I love you too," I whispered against his lips as I heard his breathing even out and he drifted off to sleep. I watched him for several more moments before turning and grabbing my clothes. Once I was clothed again I headed back to my suite and got in the shower.

As I lathered up my body I replayed the night's events in my mind. I seriously doubted mating with Nate like that was the right idea. There was no way to tell how the next few days would go as his body, mind, and emotions evened out after such a rapid growth. I just prayed he wouldn't hate me for what we did.

CHAPTER 6

I was standing over Nate's bed at the infirmary when they brought him out of the medical coma a couple of days later. After several minutes, his gorgeous eyes fluttered open. He looked around, confused, then down his body. Nate's eyes just about popped out of his head.

"I made it," he said as he looked back up to me. "I'm huge!"

I couldn't help but burst out laughing at his first reaction. Having seen hundreds of first reactions after someone's transition, Nate's was a new one. "It's all that milk you've been drinking over the years."

"Does a body good," he replied smiling at me, but then his face turned slowly into a frown. "You let me mate you."

"I did," I answered quietly, swallowing loudly. "You wouldn't drink any blood if it wasn't mine."

"I remember, but I was out of my mind at the time," he growled. "How could you let this happen?"

"It's what you said you wanted," I whispered, my eyes filling with tears.

"You should have known I wasn't in a position to know what I wanted right then," Nate yelled at me. His words echoed through the room, drawing all eyes on us.

"I didn't mate with you, you can still find your mate when you want to," I said, backing away from him.

He reached out and grabbed my arm before I could flee. "But I still have to bite you every few days," he replied. "I've been out for a few days, and that means you need my bite right now."

After a vampire mates they have to mate and be

bitten by their mate on a regular basis. I don't know the science of it, something about our genetic makeup. Once you are bitten and mated you need your mate's fangs, the compound they give off, to stay alive. It's the same compound in our saliva that helps wounds heal, but when mated our bodies start craving it. Now that he'd mated me, Nate's bite was as important to my health as food and blood.

"Yes," I said, looking anywhere but in his eyes. "I'm sorry."

"Whatever," he grumbled as he pulled me down towards him. He grabbed my hair roughly and tilted my head to the side. When his fangs sank into the side of my neck, my cock responded as it did a few days ago; instantly swelling and then exploding in my shorts. While I knew I needed his bite and it gave me relief, I felt humiliated that he did it here, like this. He drank deeply for a few moments before he released me and pushed me away.

"Did you have to do it like that?" I asked not even bothering to ask him to lick the bite closed. "In front of people like this? It's supposed to be something intimate between mates."

"You're lucky I care enough to bite you at all," he snapped, causing me to take a few steps back. I'd never seen this side of Nate before.

I closed my eyes, praying he was just upset and the transition hadn't turned him into a dickhead.

"I'm sorry, Matteo. I don't know what's going on with me, but it's like I can't hold onto one emotion. They're all swarming me."

"That's normal," I replied, falling back into instructor mode. It was easier for me to be his teacher and help him than deal with our personal crap. "You'll feel this on and off for the next month or so. Your body grew so quickly, and your hormones and organs are adjusting the new levels of chemicals your body needs to produce to keep up."

"One minute I'm so angry with you and the next I'm grateful that you willingly sacrificed yourself to mate with me so I got the blood I needed."

"We'll figure it out, Nate," I said as I took his hand. "Just don't think about it right now, okay? You're going to have enough issues, put this one on the back-burner."

"Okay, it's just..." he whispered, tears running down his cheeks.

I leaned over and gave him a chaste kiss on the lips, then let go of his hand. "What is it, Nate? You can tell me."

"You won't like it," Nate replied, trying to turn away from me.

"I don't like it now, so just tell me," I replied, raising an eyebrow as I searched his face for answers. "We can't have secrets between us. No matter what we decide or what happens, no secrets."

"Fine," he mumbled as he started playing with the infirmary blanket covering his lower body. "It's just that, if we're mated, it's for eternity. One man, the only man I've ever been with, for all the rest of my days."

"So this is about you being upset that someone better might come along?" I asked, more shocked than pissed right then.

"No!" He yelled, reaching for my hand, "it's not about finding someone better. It's just I've never played around with sex. What if it turns out I like something you don't? Hell, I don't even know what I like."

"Did you like what we did so far?" I replied, starting to get confused. "I mean we can try different things if you want."

"Even if we dabble in different stuff, there's only so much you can try with one person."

It hit me then like a ton of sharp, pointed bricks. "You want to play the field. This is about you wanting to fuck other people!"

"Well, no, maybe, yes?" He answered, looking lost and confused. "Fuck, I don't know! I'm just trying to deal with that door being closed to me for good."

"Don't worry, Nate," I said sarcastically, dropping his hand. "I'm not closing that particular door for you. Go ahead, sleep with whomever you want, just don't come knocking on my door."

"Matteo, wait!" Nate called out as I started to walk away.

I spun on my heel, completely pissed off, growling. "I knew something like this would happen. But you wouldn't listen to me, would you? Last night it was all, '*I love you*' and '*I choose you*'. Today it's you 'want to be with other people'. That's not love Nate. And now I'm stuck being mated to a man who wants to play the field. Thanks a fucking lot!"

This time I did leave, ignoring his calling after me to stop. Fuck him! I felt the tears burning in my eyes as I left the infirmary. I was so lost in my own world that I barely heard the whizzing sound. But I felt the blinding pain on the right side of my forehead. I had only seconds to realize I was falling to the ground before my world went black.

* * * *

I woke up in a bed, surrounded by people. At first I couldn't make out anything any of them were saying to me. I stared at them, trying to figure out the words as my hearing started to come back to me.

"Matteo, are you okay?" one man asked me. He was leaning over me, touching the side of my face. And while he was gorgeous, I didn't like that the stranger was touching me, even if part of me felt it was right.

"Who are you?" I asked, brushing his hand away.

"What?" he asked, his eyes going wide.

"Who are you? For that matter, where am I?"

"Matteo, you're in the infirmary," another man said from the other side of me. He looked familiar, but I couldn't put my finger on it. "You were shot, brother."

"Dimitri?" I asked, his name suddenly coming to me. "You're my brother, Dimitri."

"Yeah, I'm Dimitri, but we're not really brothers," Dimitri explained gently. "We're best friends. We've been best friends for decades."

"You keep saying Matteo, is that my name?" I asked, still confused. It was then I realized the right side of my head felt like it was blown open. "My head, fuck it hurts. I was shot in the head?"

"Yeah, buddy. You were walking out of the infirmary when a sniper bullet clipped the right side of your forehead," he answered as he sat on my bed. "You're going to have some memory loss. We don't know how much yet, but it's good you remember me, at least. It means you don't have complete amnesia."

"Okay, but who's the guy that was touching me?" I asked Dimitri before turning back to look at the man on the other side of my bed.

"That's Nate, he's your mate," Dimitri told me. I reached out and grabbed my friend's hand as my thoughts seemed to spin out of control.

"I'm Matteo and I'm mated to Nate," I said, more for myself than anyone. It seemed I needed to say it all out loud to try and get a handle on it. "And I was shot. Why was I shot?"

"That's my fault," a third man said, moving to the foot of my bed. "I'm Lance, one of your students. You challenged me and I lost. My father found out and was enraged; it seems he put a hit out on you. The sniper sat outside the camp walls and took a shot at you when you left the infirmary. People saw and rushed to you, blocking his shot I guess. That's why he only took one shot and didn't kill you."

"Okay, I'm on like info overload here," I said holding up my hand to stop him. "You're Lance. Why did I challenge you? What is a challenge?"

"All right everyone, I need you to leave," a fourth man said, stepping up to the bed. I guessed he had to be a doctor, with the white lab coat and stethoscope around his neck. "Give my patient some room, he just woke up. I need to examine him. You can all come back after the exam."

"Can Dimitri stay?" I asked the doctor. "I remember him."

"Fine," the doctor sighed, shooing away the others. When they left he started his barrage of tests and questions. It felt never-ending, and completely exhausting. The entire time, Dimitri held my hand when the doctor allowed him. It had to be at least a couple of hours before the doctor pulled up a little stool on wheels and sat by my bed.

"Your brain looks to be fully functioning, Matteo," he said smiling. "It's a miracle, really, given how the bullet entered and exited your head. But your brain seems to have healed and regenerated.

You're lucky you're a vampire, a human would have been killed instantly."

"Yeah, lucky," I snorted. "What about my memories?"

"Some may come back," he answered, tiredly rubbing his hands over his face. "Best case scenario is that they all do. We just don't know what memories were stored in that part of your brain. So far your language, motor, and finite skills don't seem to have been affected, just your memory. When dealing with the brain, nothing is exact. There's still too much about it we don't know."

"Thanks, doc," Dimitri said as he took my hand again. The doctor nodded and stood before patting my arm. I thought it was an odd thing to do, but understood it was his way of trying to comfort me. He turned and left us alone then.

"So, what now?" I asked, turning back to my friend. "I mean, I get that I'm a warrior and we're at a training facility. And I'm some type of instructor, but what do I do?"

"For now you need rest, my friend," Dimitri replied with a gentle smile.

"Wait. Please tell me why I got shot?"

"The man you met, Lance," Dimitri started to say as he sat back down. He walked me through what happened with Lance's transition, his attempted rape of Nate, and my subsequent challenge. "Lance's father is a council member and saw his son's challenge and loss as something not deserving of his high and mighty family."

"Killing me won't erase what happened," I said, still confused.

"No, but it appears he thought it was a just punishment for you after humiliating Lance," Dimitri explained, shaking his head. "It seems he didn't know Lance actually enjoyed most of it and has feelings for you. Either way, he's sitting at council headquarters in LA awaiting trial. Lance told the council he would testify against his father."

"Wow," I whistled. "That's going to be awkward."

"Probably, but whatever you said to Lance seems to have helped, along with his transition," Dimitri said as he shrugged his shoulders. "He's not the same pain in the ass we all knew and hated. It really seems he might become a good, honorable warrior."

"Great," I replied nodding. "I just wish it didn't take me getting shot and losing my memories for Lance to see the kind of monster his family is."

"True, that," Dimitri chuckled. We both turned when we heard someone clearing their throat to announce their arrival. I wasn't shocked to see it was Nate, more uncomfortable with the conversation to come. Dimitri turned back to me, "Don't stress yourself out, Matteo. You need to rest right now."

"I'll be okay," I assured my friend and patted his hand. "I got this."

He sat there a few moments longer, searching my face for something. I wasn't sure what he was looking for, but he seemed to find it. Dimitri stood, gave me a nod, then turned and walked to Nate. I couldn't hear what they were saying, but they whispered something to each other. Nate nodded a few times, then Dimitri patted him on the back and left.

I watched the six-seven, gorgeous man walk towards me. My mouth watered at the sight of him; his short, wavy blond hair and beautiful forest green eyes. I just about swallowed my tongue when he leaned over and kissed me. Melting into that kiss, I grabbed his shirt and pulled him down closer to me.

"Wow," I whispered as we broke the kiss. It seemed like those eyes were burning into my soul as he stared down at me. "So you're my mate."

"In a way," he answered with a sigh, and then sat down where Dimitri had just left. The next ten minutes or so, Nate explained about our mating and how we got where we were currently. "So yeah, that was our last conversation before you got shot."

I watched the man in front of me, not having said a word the entire time he had been talking. "So, you do want to be mated to me?"

"Yes, very much so," he answered as he raised my hand to his lips and kissed it. "It's just been a lot, with my transition. I'm confused. Does that make any sense?"

"I guess," I replied before pulling him back down for a kiss. "Until I remember, if I ever remember, I'll be in the same boat. Only having ever made love to you."

"And you're okay with that?" Nate asked, searching my face.

"I'm not sure, I just woke up after being shot and the only thing I remember is that Dimitri and I are friends. I guess sex isn't at the front of my mind right now."

"Fair enough."

"I know I don't like the idea of us playing separately if we're mated…" An idea popped into my head. "But what would you think if we maybe invited someone else to play with us?"

"You'd do that?"

"I'd try it," I answered, rubbing his hand in mine. "I'm not sure what I was into before, and I might not ever know. But if this is something you want to do, I'm willing to try it."

"Oh fuck, I'm totally picturing fucking someone while watching them suck you off," he groaned as I saw his cock grow hard under his shorts.

"I take it you like that idea, Nate," I said, then decided to be bold. I reached out and rubbed his hard-on through his shorts. He spread his legs a bit to accommodate my wandering hand. "I don't remember you, Nate, and I only know what you've told me. But I feel as if this is right, that I do know you."

"We love each other," he replied as he leaned down and kissed me again. This time I slid my tongue into his open mouth. Groaning at the taste of my mate, I wrapped my free hand behind his head and pulled him closer. When he reached under the sheet and started stroking my naked cock I just about melted into the bed.

"Prove it," I hissed. "Suck my cock."

He looked at me with wide eyes for a moment before smiling widely. Nate looked around to make sure we were alone before pulling the sheet down and lifting up my hospital gown. Without a word, he moved closer to my dick and licked off the drop of pre-cum that formed at the head of my cock. I groaned at the feeling of his tongue. Then he took the head of my dick into his mouth and started to suck on it.

"Fuck! That's it, baby," I said, wrapping my hand in his hair and guiding him down further onto my cock. He moaned around my dick and I felt the vibrations shoot through me. Without even meaning to, my hips started to pump up, gently fucking his mouth. "Take me all the way in your throat."

Nate smiled around my cock, looking straight into my eyes as he swallowed my entire length. What little control I had left snapped. I grabbed both sides of his head as I moved my hips in time with his mouth. He moved his other hand to cup and massage my balls.

"Squeeze them," I hissed out as I kept pumping my cock into his mouth. Nate did as I asked and I felt them start to draw up. "So fucking good."

He sucked harder, moving his tongue around my dick as I

fucked his face. One last squeeze to my nuts and I cried out my release as Nate swallowed every drop of my cum. My whole body shook and my vision started to swim. It hit me then that the doc probably wouldn't have wanted me to be doing any physical activity just then.

"I'm going to throw up," I said as the nausea hit me. Nate moved quickly and helped me lean over the side of the bed. We made it just as my stomach decided to empty itself. He kept rubbing my back and saying soothing words to me as I kept vomiting. When I was finally done, Nate helped me lie back down and found a cold washcloth to put on my forehead.

"Never thought anyone would have that reaction to my sucking them off," Nate mumbled.

"It wasn't that, baby. It was the getting shot earlier today," I chuckled. "I'm pretty sure you're not supposed to engage in physical activities this soon after a bullet to the head. The blow job was fantastic. I officially know what heaven is like."

"I aim to please," he replied, leaning over to kiss my lips.

"Nate," I said gently as I held onto his head, making sure he was looking right at me. "I don't have a problem with us playing with others, as long as it's together. And no one gets our asses but each other, okay?"

He seemed to think it over for a few moments, then smiled widely, "I think that's fair. You're right, I don't like the idea of someone else being in your ass."

"I feel the same way," I said pulling him down for another kiss. "I'm getting sleepy, baby."

"Okay, you get some rest, my mate," he replied, running his fingers through my hair.

Someone behind Nate cleared his throat, and when Nate

turned around I could see it was Lance. "Can I talk to Matteo for a minute before he goes to sleep?"

"I'll be fine, Nate," I told him when he looked back down at me. "You go ahead and rest up. I'll need someone to help me with my rehab."

Nate chuckled and waggled his eyebrows at me before giving me another quick kiss and leaving the room.

"I'm so sorry, Matteo," Lance said as he came towards my bed. "I never had any idea my father was serious."

"What are you talking about, Lance?"

"When my father called and asked me what happened with Nate and the challenge," Lance cried softly, hiccupping as he explained. "He said he would kill you, but I didn't think he was serious. He said he would kill you for doing that to me but I never dreamed in a million years he would really do it. I thought he was just angry and it was his rage talking. I swear if I thought it was a real threat I would have told someone..."

"It's not your fault, Lance," I replied pulling my student down towards me for a hug. "I know you truly care for me and wouldn't let someone hurt me."

"I wouldn't," he sobbed, holding onto me tightly. "Even if I hated you, what you did was right and I learned a lot from it. You didn't deserve to be killed or shot for what you did. It was dishonorable of my father to have done this. If he wanted to save face or protect our family name, he should have challenged you."

"He knew he would lose, Lance," I said, rubbing his back. The irony wasn't lost on me, I was the one who got shot, but here I was comforting Lance. "I would never blame you for your father's actions. This is not your fault, and I'm going to be just fine."

"But your memories—" I put my hand over his mouth.

"Maybe they will come back, maybe they won't. But it's worth it if you see now who your father really is," I replied, still trying to soothe him. "I have faith in you, Lance. I think the farther you are away from your family the better chance you have at becoming a great warrior and a good man."

"My father said he's going to cut me off if I testify against him," he said sitting up to look at me. "I told him to go ahead, that what he did was wrong and he needs to be held accountable for it."

"I agree, but the choice is yours."

"Thank you, Matteo," he said as he cupped my cheek. "Nate is a very lucky guy."

"Yeah, hope he realizes that," I chuckled. "Now, forgive yourself, because there's really nothing for me to forgive, Lance. And let me get some rest, I'm wiped."

He surprised me by giving me a quick kiss on the lips, "I couldn't resist. You're in no condition to stop me and I've always wondered what that would feel like."

"Get out of here before Nate finds out," I answered, shoving him away playfully. I wasn't going to yell or bitch at him for stealing a kiss.

Lance touched his fingers to his lips and smiled before turning and leaving. He started laughing as he reached the doorway and it was the first time I had faith that Lance had a chance at a real life. All he needed was someone to see past the angry boy facade and have a little faith in him.

CHAPTER 7

The next day I felt as if I were losing my mind. I was going absolutely stir crazy. The doctor and I had talked more that morning and he told me that seeing, and being in, familiar places would help me with my memories. There was nothing he could really do to help me, or guarantee they would come back, but he said immersing myself in my old life was a good first step.

"Nate, thank god! Get me the fuck out of here," I begged when my mate came to see me the next afternoon.

He stopped walking, just stood there looking me over before bursting out laughing. "Well that's one hell of a hello."

"I'm sorry," I replied sheepishly. "Hello, my wonderful mate. Now please spring me from prison."

"It's not prison," my doctor grumbled, coming up to the other side of my bed. "And I can't release you into your own care."

"Can you release him into mine?" Nate asked as he walked the rest of the way to me and took my hand. "I promise to take good care of him."

"Fine, but no more sexual activity for at least a few more days," the doctor chuckled as he reached over and grabbed a wheelchair. "He needs to lay down as much as possible or sit up only at a slight angle. Matteo's brain needs to be jarred as little as possible while he's healing."

"Done," Nate said as he helped me sit up and get into the chair. I didn't like being wheeled around, but what the doctor said made sense. So, as much as I wanted to complain right then, I wanted out of that hospital even more.

"I'll be good, I promise," I swore as Nate started to roll me out of the room.

"Yeah, and hell will freeze over," Nate hissed in my ear before sucking on my earlobe for a moment. I shivered all over, wanting to pout when he pulled away and started pushing the chair.

"I think you're going to be the problem. You can't seem to be able to keep your hands off of me," I chuckled, loving that he couldn't. Don't get me wrong, I wasn't upset, merely teasing my mate. Nate poked me in the shoulder, letting me know he took my comment in the manner it was meant.

Thankfully Nate was incredibly strong and adapted to his transition well, because the camp wasn't set up to accommodate wheelchairs. Once we were out of the infirmary he had trouble pushing me across the rocks towards the warrior housing. When we got to the house there was an elevator we could use. Most warriors rarely used it; it was actually a service elevator for the household staff.

I sighed once we got to a room that I assumed was mine, and Nate opened the door. He wheeled me in and over to the bed. Looking around, nothing struck me as familiar.

"Matteo, don't cry," Nate whispered as he knelt down in front of me. I reached up and wiped away the tears I didn't even realize I was shedding. "We'll figure this out, okay? I know your memories will come back, and even if they don't we have an eternity to make new ones."

"I just feel so lost," I whispered closing my eyes. He leaned forward and put his head on my lap while wrapping his arms around my legs. I moved my arms around him and down his back. We stayed like that for several moments before the position started to give me a headache. "Can you help me into bed? I want to lie down."

"Of course, my mate, for all the rest of my days," Nate

answered as he stood up. I froze; something about what he said haunted me. He helped me up and settled me into bed before sitting down next to me. Nate frowned at me, looking almost pissed off, and confused. The combination of what he said, and his reaction to me, loosened something inside my head.

Suddenly I was flooded with images and memories. I remembered everything from the moment Nate was out of his medical coma until I got shot. Every word, emotion, and heartbreak over ran my senses like a crazy flashback. I turned and looked at him, his eyes wide with concern, "Get out."

"Matteo, what just happened?" he asked, ignoring what I said. "You were staring off into space and not responding to me."

"I remember what happened right before I got shot," I growled. "I want you gone!"

"Please don't do this," Nate begged, looking panicked. "I told you what happened and we worked it all out."

"You telling me, and me actually remembering it, feeling it, are two very different things."

"I'm sorry," he whispered as he leaned in to kiss me. I turned my head away and he straightened back up. "I never meant to hurt you, Matteo. Right now you might not remember what your transition was like, the hurricane of emotions it is. But when you do, I hope you can forgive me for not handling mine very well."

"Just go, I want to be alone," I answered, completely exhausted.

Nate got up from the bed and walked to the door. He turned as he grabbed the knob, "I meant what I said about wanting to be mated to you. I've wanted you from the moment I met you."

"But I'm just not enough," I said before turning on my side

away from him. He left without another word and I just stared off into space. Several minutes had passed by when I heard someone at my door again. "I said I wanted to be alone."

"I don't give a fuck what you want, you stupid cocksucker," someone growled. I turned over as fast as my injured body could manage.

There stood Gabe Aretos, Lance's father, and boy did he look pissed. I knew he was a warrior before being a council member. But seeing him now, fangs and claws out, it was apparent.

The only reason I even recognized the man was that I remembered seeing him in the car when Lance was dropped off at the camp. The man hadn't even given his son's new instructors the respect of getting out of the damn car and meeting us.

"You here to finally challenge me? Or are you just going to kill a wounded man when he can't fight back?" I asked, disdain dripping off my words.

"You're not worth challenging," Gabe snarled as he stepped towards me. "You look down your nose at me? Some foreigner who comes from a nothing family?"

"I'm a warrior for our race, one of the best," I replied, trying to sit up and failing miserably at it.

"And yet you challenge a council member's son, knowing he can't win," Gabe spat at me. "There's no honor in that!"

"I was teaching him a lesson," I yelled as loud as my pounding head would allow. "One he learned quite well. Did anyone tell you why I challenged Lance?"

"Because you mate was trying to fuck him."

"I walked in on Lance trying to rape a pre-trans," I answered finally managing to sit up. "Nate wasn't my mate then. Lance attacked him right after his transition out of jealousy for our relationship."

"Bullshit," Mr. Aretos roared before smacking me across the face with his claws. "My son's no fag!"

"Yes, he is," Lance snarled as he walked through the door and grabbed his father's hand. "Even if I wasn't, this is no way to handle this. How did you even get out?"

"Money greases a lot of hands," Gabe snorted, yanking his arm away from Lance. "I'm here to finish the job and protect our family's honor."

"More like smear it," Lance yelled. "What I did was wrong. I was confused and overrun by emotions after my transition. I wanted Matteo for myself, but attacking Nate wasn't the answer. I took my punishment like a man, there's nothing dishonorable about that. But what you're doing, hiring an assassin and coming after Matteo when he's injured; there's no honor in that."

"He's warped your mind, you're not a fag," Gabe growled, turning on Lance. Seeing he was distracted, I grabbed my cell phone and called Dimitri. I left the phone on the night stand so he could hear what was going on.

Lance was still facing my direction and saw what I was doing. "Yes, I am, father. And coming here and killing Matteo won't change that."

"You're confused. You're still going through the effects of your transition," Gabe said, as if he was trying to convince himself.

"I've wanted Matteo since months before my transition," Lance replied, looking at me over his father's shoulder.

"You turned him into a fag!" Gabe turned back to me and screamed. His face was bright red with anger as he launched himself at me. Lance was just as fast, tackling his father to the ground. I watched in horror as the two of them traded blows; Lance wasn't strong enough to take on a centuries-old vampire, and ex-warrior, even if his father was out of shape and hadn't been training.

Moments later, the cavalry came. Dimitri and Alexander raced through the door, looking at me before seeing the fight on the ground. They jumped right in, pulling Gabe off a losing Lance. Alexander was easily able to restrain Gabe by himself as Dimitri went to help Lance.

"You're dead to me," Gabe screamed as Alexander started to drag him out of the room. "You are no longer my son, Lance!" He turned to me then, just before Alexander pulled him into the hallway. "And you, fag, this isn't over. I have a very long reach. Your days are numbered!"

"Shut the fuck up," Alexander growled before punching Gabe in the face. The man slumped to the floor unconscious. "Good, I'd rather deal with him this way."

"Thanks guys," I said as I flopped back to bed. "Fuck, I hate claws to the face."

"I'm sorry, Matteo," Lance gasped as Dimitri lifted him up. "I saw my father enter the camp on my way back from the mess hall. I didn't know what to do, and no one was around, so I just ran after him."

"This isn't your fault," I said taking his hand as Dimitri started to carry him out of the room. Lance was a little smaller than Dimitri, luckily, so he could handle it. "And you jumped in to save me. Thank you, Lance."

"Anytime," he mumbled as he passed out.

"He's beaten up pretty bad," Dimitri explained when I looked at him. "I'll get him to the infirmary."

"And I'll take father asshole here to our lock-up," Alexander said grabbing one of Gabe's feet and dragging him out of the room.

Dimitri and I shared a smile at Alexander's antics.

"I love my mate," he chuckled as he walked towards the door. "I'll send someone over to help you with your face."

"I'm good," I answered as I touched my already healing gashes. "I moved away in time, so I didn't get it deep."

"Okay, my friend," Dimitri nodded as he left my room. I had been exhausted before, now there wasn't a word for how tired I felt. Closing my eyes, it was moments before I was out. And boy did I ever have some intense dreams.

Somewhere in the middle of my dream I realized it wasn't made up; it was my memories.

"You shouldn't play with fire, Nate."

"I want to be burned by you," he moaned as he started to kiss the side of my neck. "Please don't deny us this anymore, Matteo."

"Fuck," I groaned as he began biting on my earlobe. I shook as his hands roamed my back, loving the feel of the smaller man finally in my arms. "Be sure this is what you want, Nate. My control is not limitless."

"Fuck me, Matteo," Nate hissed in my ear, making my cock twitch against his. "I want you pounding my ass. I need to feel your cock inside me."

In the dream I also remembered and felt what I had been feeling at that moment. The months of built-up desire, and how hard I'd tried to deny my feelings for Nate. Just then, the images sped up as if someone hit fast-forward.

"Nate, don't push me," I growled, desperately wanting to do what he said. Instead I pulled my fingers out of him and let him slide down until his feet touched the floor. "This is wrong. We can't do this."

"It's not wrong," Nate yelled, shocking me down to my core.

I'd never heard him raise his voice before, especially not to me. "Fine, I'm all stretched and ready to go. If you won't fuck me, I'm sure I can find someone else who will."

He didn't get more than two steps away from me before I was on him again. The idea of someone else touching him, especially after what we just shared, had me seeing red.

"You want me to fuck you, Nate?"

"Yes, I want you, Matteo," he panted, unable to move, seeing as I had his chest pinned against the wall. My body surrounded his smaller one completely as I held us both facing the tile. "And you want me."

"God help me, I do," I answered as I lined up my cock with his perfect little hole. Gently, I pushed in, stopping after passing the first ring. "You're so fucking tight, Nate."

"I said I wasn't a virgin," Nate seemed to have trouble talking, "I didn't say I'd had anyone in my ass before."

"I'm your first?" I asked, a thrill shooting through my entire body at the idea of being the only person in the man before me. "I should have prepared you more."

"It feels perfect, Matteo," he replied, turning to smile at me over his shoulder. "You're a perfect fit."

"Fuck," I groaned, loving that little smile of his and the fact that I was pleasing him. Not being able to hold still any longer I pushed more of my cock into him. I slowly worked it in and out of his very tight ass, grabbing his hips once I had worked more than halfway into him. "So fucking tight. Your ass is like heaven."

It was like being there again, as if it was happening for the first time. All the sensations hitting me made my cock swell and explode. Shit! I hadn't had a wet dream in centuries, but this was so much more than simply a dream. I didn't even have time to enjoy my post-orgasmic glow before moving on to what happened next.

"I'm not a mistake," Nate whispered as he started to back *away from me. "Don't do this, Matteo. Don't take this away from us."*

"There is no us, *Nate," I said firmly, knowing in my heart it was a lie. There was very much an 'us', and I wanted there to be. "This should never have happened."*

"You don't mean that."

"I do mean that, Nate," I replied, squaring my shoulders to leave no room for argument. "This was a mistake, it will never happen again. I won't ever touch you again, Nate."

"No," Nate whispered. Tears started to fall down his cheeks. Seeing the pain I was causing him made me want to do nothing but pull him into my arms and comfort him. But I knew this was best for him. Nate had so much promise, and was so young. He didn't need to be tied to a centuries-old warrior, he needed to explore life. I couldn't let him miss out on that, no matter how much I wanted him.

"I'm sorry I let this happen," I said as I got to my feet. I reached out a hand to help Nate up. He looked at it like it was a snake before his gaze went back to my eyes.

"It wasn't a mistake," he sniffled as he got to his feet without my help and backed away. "I'm not sorry it happened, so don't you dare apologize."

I woke up clutching my chest. My heart was breaking at the memory of Nate running away from me after all the shit that had come out of my mouth. And I hadn't been just out of my transition. Yeah, I had been trying to protect Nate; I remembered that part. But I still hurt him badly, no matter my reasoning. He had forgiven me, was I able to do the same?

Before I could even answer my own question, the door burst open. Nate rushed into the room and leaned over me. "My god, what did he do to you?"

"I'm fine, the scratches are healing," I replied, smiling up at him. Making the decision that I could forgive Nate, I reached out and pulled him down to me. *Fuck!* My mate knew how to kiss. Nate wasn't just some wet noodle having me do everything; he gave as well as he took. I grabbed him by the neck and pulled him down to the bed.

Nate wrapped his hands around my neck, one hand tangling in my hair. I never wanted this kiss to end. I could spend the rest of my life kissing Nate. Oh, he could kiss like no one I'd ever been with before. Nate didn't just kiss, he devoured, stealing every last breath from my lungs. Needing more, I ripped off Nate's shirt, using one claw to shred it down the middle, and pulled it off him. I let my hands wander over Nate's smooth, soft, but firm skin.

"I take it you forgive me?" He gasped as we came up for air.

Nodding for the moment while I caught my breath, Nate's wide smile warmed my heart. "I dozed off for a while and relived our time in the shower. I was such an asshole. But you had to have forgiven me if we got together and mated. If you cared enough to forgive me when I messed up, then this can't be about you not wanting me."

"It's not," he whispered against my lips, choking up. "I love you, Matteo. I don't want another mate. Forget I ever brought up anyone else. Please? I swear I'll never bring it up again."

"Shhh, baby, calm down," I said when I realized he was about to hyperventilate. He wrapped his arms around me and for the moment we just held each other. When I felt him calming down I decided to try again. "I'm still okay with us trying to bring someone else to our bed, Nate. It's just hard to relive these memories. It's not just like remembering something that happened to me, I'm living it for the first time."

"I'm not sure I understand," Nate replied. He moved up so he could look down at my face, confusion written all over his.

"I know I'm remembering things that have happened to me," I explained, trying to find the words. "But it's more like it's really happening to me then, for the first time, as I'm remembering it. And as if I'm getting hit upside the head with a baseball bat at the same time."

Nate searched my face for a minute, running his hand over the uninjured side of my face. Then he did one of the hottest things ever. He leaned down and licked my claw wounds, along with the blood on my face. I moaned and held onto his arms as I squirmed in ecstasy. Not only was his saliva healing me, it was amazingly erotic.

"I want you to claim me as I did you, Matteo," he whispered when he was done. Nate looked deep into my eyes when he said it, then tilted his head to expose his neck to me. My fangs were instantly out and my cock hard.

"That's what I wanted to talk to you about," I said gently, taking his head in my hands. "I didn't want to bring someone else to our bed without completing our mating."

"Great minds think alike," Nate smiled, and gave me a peck on the lips. "I feel the same way. We might end up playing around with someone else, but you're my mate. You're the mate I want for all eternity and nothing will ever change that." He tilted his head again for me, but then looked back at me.

"What's wrong Nate?"

"When I heard you were hurt, that Mr. Aretos tried to kill you again and I wasn't here. I-I freaked, Matteo," he explained as a single tear escaped his eyes. "The thought of never holding you again, not being able to apologize, was too much for me. I can't lose you, Matteo. I won't risk this, not for anyone else or any threesome. I love you. You're never allowed to die and leave me."

I chuckled at what he said at the end there, and pulled him down to me. "I can't promise I'll never die, but I'm not going anywhere, Nate. And I'm fine with playing around, as long as it's always together, and not just an excuse to cheat."

"I don't want to cheat, or be with anyone else," Nate said adamantly. "I just want to try new things, but with you."

"Then let me claim you, my mate," I whispered before licking the side of his neck. Nate moved his head to give me better access and I sank my fangs into him. The blood that rushed into my mouth and over my tastebuds was heaven. It was incredibly sweet, like maraschino cherries. I almost laughed when I realized it gave a whole new meaning to having a sweet tooth.

A moment later Nate bit me as well, causing us to both moan loudly. My cock swelled as I felt his do the same. Several more pulls on his neck, and I climaxed. I lifted my head to roar out my release at the same time Nate did. We held onto each other tightly, riding out our orgasms and the pure bliss of completing the mating bond.

"Wow, that was intense," Nate said in my head. I pushed him up a bit so I could look into his eyes.

"It was fucking amazing," I replied, smiling when Nate's eyes went as wide as saucers.

"Holy shit," he whispered before leaning down and attacking my lips. We made out for several minutes before my head started to spin and I pulled away. "Dizzy?"

"Yeah, sorry," I said as I snuggled up to his side.

"Nothing to apologize for," he snickered and wrapped an arm around me. "I can't stop smiling. We're really mated."

"And I've never been happier," I replied, right before I yawned.

"Me, too," Nate said, then kissed my head. "Get some rest, my love. I don't like you being injured."

I felt a smile play across my lips as I drifted off to sleep. It was probably bad of me to hope I didn't have any more memories float to the surface, but I did anyways. Remembering was very traumatic and took a lot of my strength, even when it happened in sleep. And right now, I just needed some rest.

CHAPTER 8

The week after I was shot the doctors finally said I could get back into my routine, and since I hadn't yet remembered what that was, Dimitri agreed to help me out. Though I was on light duty only, at least I could get back to training the post-trans. After an hour in my office, which I had to be told how to find, I was ready to shoot myself in the head.

It's one thing when you have horrible handwriting you can read. But when you don't remember what your handwriting looks like, you can't make out your own chicken scratch. I guess I'd been set in my centuries-old ways, since I never seemed to put anything on the laptop I had.

"Son of a bitch," I yelled, and threw the schedules I couldn't figure out. Leaning back in my desk chair I started rubbing my temples.

"Come on, Matteo, let's go for a run," Dimitri said from the doorway. "It's your favorite way to clear you head."

"Good thing one of us knows that," I grumbled as I stood and walked around my desk. Still cussing under my breath, I bent over, picked up the schedules, and put them back on my desk.

"It'll get better, man," Dimitri patted me on the back as we left my office. I followed him out to 'our favorite track'. And I knew the pressure in my head wasn't from my injury; it was pure stress.

When we got to the track and started jogging I felt the headache start to fade. The faster I picked up the pace, the better I felt. Dimitri grabbed my arm, slowing me down, "Light duty, Matteo. Let's not overdo it your first time out, okay?"

"Yeah, sorry," I replied, slowing down. He was right; I felt my muscles start to burn. It was just, for the first time in days, I wasn't pissed off that I couldn't remember. I didn't feel lost and confused. Realizing that made me stop in my tracks and turn to my best friend, "What if I never remember, Dimitri? What if I'm never again the man I was?"

"The man you are is ingrained in you, Matteo," he said after a moment. "What you've experienced in life made you the man you are. And while you might not ever remember the life that got you here, you're still here. Nothing can change that man."

"I hope you're right, brother," I answered as we started jogging again. "Thanks for all the help."

"You may not remember all the times you've been there for me, my brother, but I do."

We kept running for another mile before I decided to broach the other subject that was weighing on me. "Have you and Alexander ever thought of bringing another person to your bed?"

"Why? Are you offering?" he laughed. Dimitri stopped running and grabbed his side, he was laughing so hard. "You do have a nice ass."

"Oh fuck you, I was being serious, you dick," I chuckled as I pushed him. He fell on his ass, still laughing hysterically. "I've been the only man Nate's ever been with, and he wants to experience all the facets of sex. We agreed, now that we're completely mated, to bring a third into the mix."

"And you're cool with that?" he asked me as he stood, his eyes wide with shock.

"I'm willing to try it," I shrugged. We were quiet a few minutes as we started jogging again. "I told him I reserve the right to change my mind if I end up not liking it. But honestly, the idea of us playing together with a third gets me hot."

"Who's the third?"

"That's part of the problem," I sighed. "How exactly do you approach someone about that? I mean, put up some flyers in the mess hall?"

"No, I wouldn't do that," he laughed and punched me in the arm. "I'd talk to Rune. But I've got to warn you, he's into some kinky ass sex."

"You hooked up with him, right?" I waited for Dimitri to nod before continuing. "What do you mean by kinky ass sex?"

"Spankings, very rough play, lots of pain," he answered as we started to slow for a cool down. "He doesn't like to be stretched out and prepared, he likes the feeling of almost being ripped apart."

"Yikes!" I gasped making a face to Dimitri. "I'm not sure Nate and I are up for that."

"Probably not," he chuckled as we stopped and started stretching. "But you said Nate wanted to experience the full array of sex."

"Good point, thanks, man," I said as we finished up. We bumped fists before it was time to take off. "Hey, keep this between us, okay?"

"You got it, brother from another," he smirked as he jogged back towards the main gym.

I headed back towards my room to find Nate. Since our mating we'd moved our stuff into one of the bigger rooms. Even if we hadn't been able to play much since I'd been shot, I liked waking up with Nate. It felt right to start the day intertwined together.

"Hey, baby," I said to Nate as I opened the door to our room. I walked over and gave him a quick kiss on the lips.

"Mmm, you smell like sweat, and manly Matteo," he purred as

he tried to pull me onto his lap.

"I'm glad you like," I chuckled. I dodged away from him and grabbed a towel as I walked into the bathroom. "I talked to Dimitri about us deciding to bring a third to our bed."

"What did he say?" Nate asked apprehensively. "Does he hate me?"

"No, not at all," I answered as I turned on the water and started to shower. "He suggested Rune. I thought we might stop by his room after I shower and change."

"We don't have to do this," Nate said as he joined me in the shower. "I'm perfectly happy with just the two of us making love together."

"I know," I nodded as I turned and helped suds him up as he did the same to me. If we kept this up, we'd either be overly horny by the time we got to Rune's room or we'd never even make it there. "The more I've thought about it, the more I like the idea too. So, let's try it. It might end up not being our thing, but I'm willing to try it."

"As long as no one gets in this sweet ass but me," Nate purred as he ran his hands over my butt. Then suddenly he pulled his hands away and started washing his hair. "We'd better hurry, otherwise I'm going to end up fucking you into the wall of the shower."

"Not that I'd object," I snickered as I finished rinsing. I hopped out of the shower and started to dry off. As I got dressed I knew that I should warn Nate about Rune's idea of sex. But at the same time, I didn't want to sound as if I was trying to talk him out of this.

"God you're hot," Nate said as he came into the room completely naked.

"I was thinking the same thing about you," I laughed as I threw him a shirt. "Now come on, let's go play."

"Fuck, I'm hard enough to pound nails," he grumbled as he quickly pulled on clothes and shoes. When we were both dressed we left the room and headed for Rune's. The entire walk there Nate was either groping or kissing some part of my body.

"You really are turned on by this, aren't you?" I asked, turning to face him a few feet from Rune's door.

"Maybe I'm fucked in the head," he answered holding my face in his hands. "But the idea of watching someone else suck that gorgeous cock of yours just flat does it for me. I'm not sure if it's a voyeur thing, or what, but it's like my ultimate fantasy."

"Okay, but if, at any time, either of us decides we don't want to do this, we say something. Deal?"

"Deal," Nate whispered before kissing me. "I love you, Matteo."

"I love you too, Nate," I said before turning and leading us the last few feet to Rune's door. I knocked quickly before my nerves gave out. Between being nervous as all hell, and Nate's large hands massaging my ass, my heart was racing so fast I thought it might jump out of my chest.

"Hang on," Rune called out, before something crashed onto the floor on the other side of the door. There was a few scrambling around sounds that had me raising an eyebrow. The door flew open and there stood a panting Rune trying to tie his robe around him. "Hi, what's up, guys?"

"You okay, Rune?" I asked glancing around him. It wasn't hard. Rune was a good looking guy, but he was pretty short for a warrior. I'd say he was under six feet and not even two twenty. But he was solid, ripped muscle; his muscles had muscles that were ripped. He had longish jet black hair that he always tied at the nape of his neck, and violet eyes.

"Yeah, fine, Matteo," he replied not meeting my gaze. "What can I do for you guys?"

"Can we come in?" Nate asked as he looked down the hall. "This isn't a conversation for others to overhear."

"Yeah, sure," Rune answered stepping back from the door and letting us enter. He looked completely puzzled as he closed the door behind us. I went and sat at the desk chair as Nate leaned against the desk next to me. Rune walked over to the bed, sat down, and cried out. He jumped back up, still moaning, and turned bright red.

Nate and I shared a look before moving towards Rune and standing on either side of him. I leaned in and whispered in Rune's ear, "Did we interrupt you playing with some toys, Rune?"

"Umm, yeah, kind of," Rune mumbled. "I forgot it was in there when I sat down. You guys threw me for a loop showing up here."

"Sorry, we didn't mean to disturb you," Nate said as he reached for the tie of Rune's robe. "We just want to join you."

"Wait… what?" Rune asked looking at me then Nate. "I thought you guys were mated?"

"We are," I answered holding Nate's hand still. I didn't want him touching Rune to affect the man's decision. "We want to play with a third, we thought of you. Are you interested?"

"Both of you want to play with me?" he whispered as his eyes just about bugged out of his head. "Yeah, I'm in."

"Good," I hissed as I let go of Nate's hand and licked the side of Rune's neck. "We want to play and explore, but we're not sure if this is what we want all the time. Are you good with a one-time deal, Rune?"

"Yes, master," Rune moaned as Nate got his robe off. I took a step back and ripped off my clothes. "May I suck your cock, master?"

"Get on the bed first, Rune," Nate growled as he almost shredded his clothes trying to get them off. Rune did as he was told and I moved towards the foot of the bed to feed him my dick. Nate's gasp took my attention. "What is this in your ass, Rune?"

"A dildo," he mumbled, turning bright red again.

"I've never seen a toy like this," Nate replied, gesturing me to come look. Intrigued I moved around Rune to see what Nate was talking about.

"Fuck, Rune," I whispered as I saw why Nate was freaked. It wasn't a normal dildo. It was small, but had plastic hook-like catches on it. Rune hadn't gotten very far pushing it into himself, which explained why he screamed when he sat on the bed. "Rune, this would tear you up inside."

"I like the pain," Rune answered, looking at us over his shoulder. "I was trying something new. I didn't know you'd be coming by. I get lonely."

My heart broke for Rune, seeing this side of him. I couldn't remember much of Rune, or anyone else, yet but I was pretty sure I'd never known this about him before.

"Can I take this out, Rune?" Nate asked as he looked at me. "I want to fuck you while you blow my mate."

"Yes, master, anything you want," Rune replied as he lowered his upper body down to the bed. Nate moved lightening quick and pulled Rune back towards the middle of the bed. He yelped in surprise and shivered. Nate gently started to remove the torturous toy as Rune cried out and shook harder. "Oh fuck, it's so much better when you do it to me than when I did it myself."

"I don't want to hurt you, Rune," Nate said gently, sadness written all over his face as he tried to ease the dildo out of Rune's ass.

"I like the pain, master," Rune moaned as he tried to push back to get the dildo back in. Nate was quicker and yanked it the rest of the way out. Rune screamed loudly and I was about to ask if he was okay, but I saw the pure bliss written over the man's face. Nate threw the toy across the room like it was a snake.

"We need to stretch you out," I said as I reached for the lube.

"Please don't, master," Rune begged. "I'm lubed up. I want you both to hurt me. Please, be rough, hit me, spank me!"

"It's up to you, Nate," I said as I moved to the foot of the bed. I raised Rune up on his hands and knees. Nate eyed me before turning back to the ass in front of him. He swatted Rune's ass a few times, shock all over his face as Rune writhed in pleasure. But then his expression changed to lust. Nate massaged his hand print on Rune's butt.

"You like that, Rune?" he asked before smacking his ass a few more times.

"Yes, master. Harder please," Rune begged, then looked up at me. "May I suck your cock, master?"

"Open wide, Rune," I said, loving that Nate was getting all hot. When he did, I guided my cock into Rune's mouth. He greedily started sucking on me like I was his last meal.

"Oh fuck that's hot," Nate groaned from the other end of Rune. "You're going to suck his cock while I pound into your ass, Rune."

Rune's only response was to moan loudly around my dick, sending wonderful vibrations through it. I grabbed his head and started fucking his face. The noises Rune made told me he loved the rough play.

"Nate, fuck him already," I said between my teeth. "I'm not going to last long; he's really good at this."

Nate nodded and grabbed the bottle of lube I'd dropped, then greased up his dick. I watched as he lined up his cock with Rune's hole and shoved it in. It was hot. Nate didn't start slow, instead fucking Rune with everything he had.

"He's so tight," Nate moaned as he slapped Rune's ass a few more times. "Yeah, Rune, suck my mate's cock."

I bit my lip, trying not to come. Between Nate's words and Rune's hot mouth, it was hard. We worked out a good rhythm, both of us pushing into Rune at the same time. His whole body was shaking like crazy as Nate and I fucked him. I pulled out of his mouth, afraid I would come too soon.

"Harder, master," Rune hissed as he looked back at Nate. "Use your claws on me."

Nate didn't seem to hear. Instead he fucked Rune like a mad man while eyeing me over. "What do you want, Nate?"

"Blow your load in his mouth," he panted as he fucked Rune into the bed. "I want to fuck him onto your dick. It's like I'm pleasing you both."

"You are, baby," I smiled as I put my cock back into Rune's mouth. "Fuck him harder, Nate."

Nate smiled widely, fangs and all, as he leaned forward. I met him halfway and kissed him as he kept thrusting into Rune. Nate groaned when my tongue got nicked on one of his fangs. I grabbed the back of his head and held him to me while our tongues dueled in each other's mouths. When I let him go, we were both gasping for air.

"I'm coming, Rune," I cried out seconds before shooting my seed down his throat. The entire time I was climaxing, I watched Nate's face. The feral look on his face as he fucked and smacked Rune's ass was what kept my orgasm going. I swear I must have come more than once, it went on so long. As my spent cock slipped from Rune's mouth, I had an idea.

Smiling at Nate, I crawled around them until I was at Nate's back. His eyes never left me until he had to turn his neck too far to see me. "What are you doing, my mate?"

"Claiming this sweet body," I purred as I licked the side of his neck while reaching around and pinching his nipples. "I want to sink my fangs into you while your monstrous cock his in his ass."

"Yes," Nate hissed as he thrust his hips forward even harder. I nibbled on his neck, teasing him. "Please, Matteo, I'm almost there. Claim me!"

Smiling as Nate begged, I pulled his head roughly to the side and sank my teeth into his soft flesh. He roared loudly as he went stiff in my arms. I drank down my mate's life essence and Nate's orgasm rocked throughout him. I was totally, completely, and forever addicted to the man in my arms.

Rune cried out under Nate just as I lifted my head and licked my bite marks. Before I could even move, Nate reached back and dragged me around the front of him. Rune had collapsed face down on the bed and Nate pulled me on top of Rune. He leaned down and licked my neck before biting me. I screamed, half in shock at his move, and half in pleasure as my cock filled and exploded again.

"Yes, fuck yes," I cried out as Nate grabbed my cock and stroked me as he drank deeply from my neck. When he was done, I felt bad we had done this on top of Rune. We started laughing as we rolled off of the poor man. I looked at Rune when I was next to him. "Are you okay?"

"Never better, master," he smiled as his eyes started to close. "Your mate is an animal. I'll play with you both anytime."

Nate turned bright red at the compliment and got off the bed. He quickly pulled on his clothes and tossed me mine. "I think this might have been a one-time deal, Rune. We wanted to try something new, but I'm not sure it's for us."

"Did I not please you, master?" Rune asked looking almost panicked as he moved to the edge of the bed. "Just order me as you wish and I will do it."

Seeing the look on Nate's face, I decided to step in. I knelt on the edge of the bed, so I was eye level with Rune and kissed him gently on the lips. "It's not you, Rune. You're hot. I think it's just that the type of sex you're into is a bit much for us. I'm not comfortable with being called master. And we pretty much ignored you, I'm sorry about that."

"Don't be sorry, I'm used to that," Rune said quietly before he jumped off the bed, grabbed his robe and raced out of the room.

"Wait, Rune," Nate said as he tried to stop the man. But Rune ducked him and kept going. "Well, shit, that didn't work out as I had wanted."

"What I said was how you felt, though, right?" I asked as I dressed. "I mean, that isn't what you're into?"

"No, it's not," Nate shook his head and ran his hand through his hair. "Rune's hot, and I loved fucking him while he sucked you off, but..."

"I'm not into the whole master thing either," I finished for him when he paused. I left my shirt off and held it in my hand as I moved towards Nate. I tilted my head up and kissed him deeply. "But it was hot watching you fuck someone while never taking your eyes off me."

"Maybe we'll try it again, just not with Rune," Nate said as he took my hand. We walked out of the room, closing the door behind us as we headed back to our room in silence. Once we were there, and the door closed behind us, Nate led me over to the bed. "Did you know Rune was into that? I mean the whole D/s thing, and that much pain?"

"Dimitri said he was into pain and rough stuff," I answered shaking my head. "But I didn't have a clue it went that far."

"I thought subs, real submissives, don't do anything without commands?" Nate asked as he pulled me to lie down next to him. "I mean, he was really forward for a sub, or is that just me?"

"I don't think there are real rules for the lifestyle," I answered as I ran my fingers through his hair. "I think there's something else going on with Rune. That wasn't a dildo I've ever seen before. It looked more like a torture device."

"It scared the shit out of me," Nate said in between kissing my chest. "Rune's always struck me as such a take-charge, has all his shit together, kind of guy. It was shocking to see this other side of him. I mean, he looked so defeated and sad when he left the room. I didn't know what to do."

"I don't know either, but I might talk to Dimitri about it," I replied, having already thought of Nate's concerns myself. His hand rubbed my chest as I kept playing with his hair. In no time I heard Nate's breathing even out and that cute snore he had start. I felt myself begin to drift as a smile spread across my face; I realized I felt closer to Nate than ever before after we played with someone else in our bed. And I had been worried it might be the end of us.

CHAPTER 9

A few days after our fun, but confusing, time with Rune I was working with Nate and Lance. They were the only new post-transitions we had training for their warrior test. While I might not remember my training, it remembered me. Either it was so ingrained in me it wasn't possible to forget, or I just didn't need the memories to keep the skills.

"Make him come to your right, Lance," I called out as they sparred with swords. "You're right handed and stronger there, if he comes to your right, it's his weaker side. Use that!"

"How do you *make* him do anything?" Lance growled as he kept countering Nate's blows. Lance was my height, so Nate had a few inches on him, and was using it to his advantage.

"Hold up guys," I said as I jogged over to them. When they moved apart I got into a fighting position with Nate. "Do the same moves you were with Lance, Nate."

He smiled widely at me, as if he really thought he had a chance in the world of beating me. Then he raised his sword up high and brought it down on top of my head, using his height advantage. Instead of just blocking the blow as Lance had been doing, I pushed back up against Nate. Which caused him to lose the center of his balance and his sword to slide off mine and fall below our waists. In a flash I had my sword to his neck, winning the fight.

"The best defense is sometimes a good offense," I said to Lance, turning back towards him. "By allowing Nate to get a false sense of winning I was able to switch up the play and attack while defending his blow. He was biding his time, tiring you out by making you constantly exert more energy to block him. If he had kept his attacks lower they wouldn't have worn you out as quickly as it takes less energy to block them when you don't have to raise your arms overhead."

"I thought it was a good plan," Nate grumbled as I lowered my sword from his neck.

"It was, baby," I chuckled. "But you have to remember the old saying; the bigger they are, the harder they fall. If you rely only on your height advantage you'll lose against a skilled warrior. To win any fight you have to keep your opponent guessing. You weren't ready for my counter and I was able to trip you up, winning the match."

"Does that mean you're going to fuck me now?" Nate whispered in my ear, sending chills down my spine. "I'll gladly lose every time if it got your fine cock in my ass."

"Behave, Nate," I growled back at him, letting him know his words affected me.

"Don't stop on my account," Lance chuckled drawing our attention. He gestured down to his hard-on in his shorts. "I'd love to watch, or join in."

"Join in?" Nate and I said at the same time. I wasn't sure about Nate, but I was completely shocked at what Lance said.

He smiled as he approached us, "I'd gladly join you guys anytime you'd let me. I told you I'd do anything to get your dick in my ass again, Matteo. Nate's hot. I'll suck him off while you fuck me."

Nate growled loudly, and I turned to calm him down. I was surprised to see lust, not anger, on his face. "I take it you like the idea, baby?"

"Yes," he hissed as he moved forward and claimed my mouth. The kiss was full of heat as he rubbed his hard cock against my stomach. "As long as I don't have to hurt him or anything like before."

"Before?" Lance asked, raising an eyebrow. "I didn't know

you guys played?"

"We have once," I said, trying not to laugh as Nate kept humping me. He'd moved me in front of him, facing Lance, as he kept pushing his cock against my ass. "The third was into things we weren't, like pain, and submission."

"I don't think I'm into that," Lance rubbed his chin, deep in thought. "I like a little bite of pain, and some burning, but nothing major."

"Matteo," Nate hissed in my ear as he nibbled on it, all the while holding onto my hips as he dry humped my ass. "Please say yes, my mate."

"We don't allow anyone to fuck us except each other, Lance," I said. I was desperately trying to focus on the conversation at hand, instead of Nate's attack on my senses. Looking around, I saw that no one was nearby to see us. We were in the back woods in one of the practice rings.

"I'm good with that," Lance hissed as he started rubbing himself through his shorts. "Anything you guys say, I'll do if I get to be with you both."

"Then suck my mate's cock," I said as Nate growled slightly against my neck.

Lance's eyes went wide before he smiled. He sauntered over as I moved out from in front of Nate. Lance got on his knees in front of my mate and pulled down his shorts. Nate's eleven inch, fully hard cock bounced out and slapped against his stomach. Lance grabbed it and licked the head, moaning loudly as Nate looked at me with an almost feral gaze.

"Baby, get down on your knees. Lance, on all fours."

Both men quickly complied, losing the rest of their clothes in the process. I shed my shirt and shorts as well, chuckling when we were all naked except for our sneakers. Moving behind Lance I had a perfect view of my mate getting head. I pulled the cheeks of Lance's ass back to reveal his pink puckered hole. Leaning forward, I swiped my tongue over it. Lance shook and Nate groaned.

"I like watching that," Nate said as I did it again. "And I know how talented that tongue of yours is, my mate."

"Want to help me?" I smirked. Nate snarled as he pulled out of Lance's mouth and moved next to me.

"Was I doing something wrong?" Lance asked, looking over his shoulder at us.

"No, we just want to rim your hole together," Nate snickered before leaning over and licking Lance's ass. "He tastes different than you do, Matteo."

"Let me taste," I purred as I leaned forward and slid my tongue into Nate's mouth. When we moved apart, we moved down to Lance's ass and both started to lick his hole.

"Oh fuck, you guys are going to kill me," Lance moaned as we continued to open up his ass with our tongues. "Please, fuck me already!"

"I think he's talking to you, my mate," Nate snickered as he sat back on his feet.

"Lube up my cock, baby," I hissed as I moved so Nate could get under me. He did so willingly, swallowing me all the way down his throat. I'd have to remember to not bring lube with us more often. I started to fuck Nate's mouth as I fucked Lance's hole with my tongue. All three of us moaned loudly and I couldn't take the foreplay anymore.

"I was just getting started," Nate whined as I pulled out of his mouth.

"Yeah, you're too good at it, baby," I chuckled as I moved my hips flush with Lance's. "Now, go get your dick sucked."

"If you insist," Nate sighed dramatically as he moved around in front of Lance. When he was ready, we nodded at each other and pushed into Lance at the same time. It seemed to drive him on overload, having both Nate and I inside of him. He went nuts, impaling himself on my cock then moving forward to deep throat Nate. I looked at my mate, his expression mirroring my own shock.

"I think we unleashed a sex machine," I groaned as Lance thrust back onto my cock.

"Let's see how much he can take," Nate smirked and grabbed Lance's head. I mirrored my mate and grabbed Lance's hips, holding him still as Nate and I plunged into him together. He moaned loudly and started shivering all over. I made sure to hit Lance's sweet spot with every thrust into his tight ass.

"Oh fuck!" Lance screamed as he pulled his mouth off Nate's cock.

"Why did he stop sucking on you?" I grunted as I kept thrusting into the man under me.

"Fangs. Came. Out," Lance panted as I fucked him. "Didn't. Trust. My. Control."

I leaned over and wrapped my arms around Lance's chest and waist. Pulling him up against my chest so we were on our knees, I met Nate's heated gaze over Lance's shoulder. Lance screamed as the angle changed and I plunged deeper into him.

Nate moved forward and started stroking Lance's cock. "Matteo's dick feels good pounding into your ass, doesn't it, Lance?"

"Yes," he hissed, shaking all over again. "Please don't stop."

"We won't," I answered, winking at Nate. "We're going to give you so much pleasure you'll pass out, Lance."

"Oh fuck," Lance screamed as he stiffened up, and then started shooting his seed all over Nate's hand. After several shots of cum from his dick, Lance went limp.

"You really fucked him into passing out," Nate chuckled as he leaned forward and kissed me. "Now shove that cock into me."

"Gladly," I growled as I pulled out of Lance and gently laid him down on the ground. Without another word, I pounced on Nate. He laughed as we rolled each other over a few times. Finally, he conceded and stopped struggling under me, then pulled his knees up to his chest. "I have to stretch you out, baby."

"I already did when Lance was sucking on me," Nate winked up at me. My eyes just about rolled into the back of my head when I saw his hole was stretched and lubed up for me. "I knew my nympho mate would need more than one ass to fuck."

I quickly lined up my cock and pushed it into Nate's tight hole. We both groaned when I bottomed out. "All those lustful looks you were giving me turned me into an animal," I said as I started to pull back out. Thrusting my hips forward, I slammed back in as hard as I could.

"Yeah, just like that, Matteo," Nate groaned as his fangs came out. "Fuck me and bite me, my mate."

"Anything to make my mate happy," I snickered as I started to fuck him like I never had anyone before. Animal was a good way to describe my behavior, machine might have worked too. I'd settle for a man possessed. Knowing I was the one giving Nate what he wanted drove me to new heights of fierce. "You're so tight, I love it."

"Fuck, you're a sex machine, Matteo," Nate grunted as I pounded into him. He tilted his head to the side as he moaned his pleasure. Not about to pass up the offering, I leaned down and sank my fangs into the soft flesh of his neck. Nate screamed louder than I had ever heard him before, "I'm coming!"

Seconds later the space between us filled with his cum as I drank down his sweet life essence. The muscles in Nate's ass clamped down on my cock, throwing me over the edge. I kept pushing my dick into the vise-tight grip of my mate's hole as I came. Lifting up my head, I roared out my orgasm. It seemed to go on for eternity as Nate's hands roamed by body.

As I came down from my climax I fell to his side, not wanting to put my full weight on him. Both of us were panting, trying to control our heart rates as we held onto each other. We were laying there in after sex bliss when I heard laughter. I looked up to see several warriors surrounding us with shit eating grins on their faces.

"Do you give lessons?" Yuri asked trying to keep a straight face. "I've always wanted to learn from a *sex machine*."

"Nate, I didn't know you could scream that loud," Dimitri snorted. "I always thought you were so quiet."

"Did you really rim Lance?" Someone else from the group called out.

"That's one way to get a student to behave," Alexander chuckled as he pointed to a passed out Lance. "Fuck him into compliance."

"You guys are just jealous you don't have a mate that can pleasure you like Matteo can," Nate said with a smug grin on his face. "My mate takes me places you guys can only dream of."

"Good point, I am jealous," Alexander nodded. "My mate can't fuck two men into bliss like that in a row."

"Excuse me?" Dimitri yelled, his eyes going wide. He stormed the few steps to his mate and towered over Alexander.

Nate laughed when Alexander put a hand on his hip and smirked at Dimitri. "Did I stutter, my love?"

"No, but you'll be making all kinds of new noises when I'm done with you!" Dimitri snarled as he landed his shoulder in Alexander's stomach and threw the smaller man over his shoulder. It was lucky they were both extremely strong since Alexander was only a few inches shorter than Dimitri. Not exactly conducive for carrying one another. "I'll show you a sex machine, Alexander. You won't be able to sit the fuck down for weeks."

"Promises, promises," Alexander snorted from over Dimitri's shoulder. He looked at me and winked as Dimitri started jogging back to their room.

I rolled my eyes and pulled my mate closer, trying to move the larger man beneath me to hide his naked body from all the onlookers. I could feel Nate's slight laughter shaking the man's chest and glanced down at him. Joy filled me, overcoming my ability to be angry with my friends. I held my mate in my arms and that was all that mattered.

The End

ALSO BY JOYEE FLYNN:

Warrior Camp
Love's Deceit
Love's Indecision

Wolf Harem Series
Second Chance Bite
Spencer's Secret (Coming Soon)

North American Dragon Series
Dragon Mine

Marius Brothers Series
Micah
Remus
Stefan (Coming Soon)

Hounds of Hell Series
Avoiding Hell's Gates

With Stormy Glenn:

Delta Wolf Series
Chameleon Wolf
Mating Games
Blood Lust (Coming Soon)

CPSIA information can be obtained at www.ICGtesting.com
Printed in the USA
240197LV00001B/261/P

9 781453 848753